D1611942

BUFFALO
FLATS

BUFFALO
FLATS

MARTINE LEAVITT

MARGARET FERGUSON BOOKS
HOLIDAY HOUSE · NEW YORK

Margaret Ferguson Books

Copyright © 2023 by Martine Leavitt
All rights reserved
HOLIDAY HOUSE is registered in the U.S. Patent and
Trademark Office.
Printed and bound in February 2022 at Maple Press, York, PA, USA.
www.holidayhouse.com
First Edition
1 3 5 7 9 10 8 6 4 2

Library of Congress Cataloging-in-Publication Data

Names: Leavitt, Martine, 1953- author.
Title: Buffalo flats / by Martine Leavitt.
Description: First edition. | New York City : Margaret Ferguson Books,
Holiday House, 2023. | Audience: Ages 12 and up | Audience:
Grades 10-12. | Summary: "The coming of age story of Rebecca
Leavitt as she searches for her identity in the Northwest
Territories of Canada"— Provided by publisher.
Identifiers: LCCN 2022016975 | ISBN 9780823443420 (hardcover)
Subjects: CYAC: Identity—Fiction. | Northwest Territories—
History—19th century—Fiction. | Christian life—Fiction.
LCGFT: Christian fiction. | Novels.
Classification: LCC PZ7.B3217 Bu 2023 | DDC [Fic]—dc23
LC record available at https://lccn.loc.gov/2022016975

ISBN: 978-0-8234-4342-0 (hardcover)

In honor of Thomas Rowell Leavitt
1834–1891

To his credit, he built well—not so much
his crude pioneer log cabins,
but his family traditions of togetherness
and integrity.
— Dr. Clark T. Leavitt

BUFFALO
FLATS

THE SIT, 1890

Rebecca had heard her father and others call this land God's country often enough that she wasn't as surprised as she might have been to come upon him, one warm spring evening, sitting on the tor overlooking Buffalo Flats. He was dressed in his work clothes, but you knew God when you saw him. A sparrow swooped over him as if everything were usual. An insect lighted on him and flew away, as if it hadn't just landed on God.

He saw her and smiled and said, "Rebecca."

She sat beside him on a large, flat rock and gazed with him at the Rocky Mountains, twenty miles to the west, sweeping straight up out of the prairie. The sun perched on the peak of Black Bear Mountain, burning like a candle, its light filling the valley like honey, golding up every solid thing: cows, cabins, barns, fields. The land looked less lonesome this way, but Rebecca loved it in all its ways—its winds and weathers, its rocky bones jutting out of the earth in places, the long-limbed prairie that stretched one's soul out of shape to see its distances.

"Buffalo Flats," Rebecca said, gesturing to the valley before them. She wondered briefly who had named the valley, and what God thought of the names people made up for his creations.

"And where are the buffalo?" he asked gently.

She didn't feel as if she were expected to answer — she supposed all questions were rhetorical with God. He would know that the buffalo had been killed off before her people arrived. But there had been a note of sadness in his voice.

Perhaps it might provide some comfort if she drew his attention to her father's caramel-colored cows grazing on the flats.

"Father's cows," she said, pointing.

He nodded with interest. It occurred to her that he would know cows, having made them in the first place. And she guessed these pilgrim cows weren't much comfort if you wanted buffalo.

Or perhaps God thought, as she did, that the land — the mountains, the prairie — was unspeakably beautiful, even without buffalo.

"Good job, sir," she said meekly.

The peaks of the Rocky Mountains seemed to look down on her like venerable ancestors in the deepening light, stern and mildly disapproving, reminding her to watch her manners.

The book of Hebrews said it was a terrifying thing to fall into the hands of the living God, but she thought sitting beside him on a rock was a comfortable thing. It might have been a long time or a short time that they sat quiet together, the sun sinking behind the peaks, the sky becoming a stained-glass window.

Rebecca recalled her mother's admonition not to be long

on her wander. She hesitated, and then decided it would go harder on her to displease Mother than to dismiss herself from the company of deity. So she said, "Guess I'll go home now."

She stood.

"Guess I will, too," he said, but it was so kindly said, it might have been, "I wish it could be longer."

She had gone only a few steps down the slope when the mountains snuffed out the sun and filled the flats below with shadow. A wolf howled from the timber, and the pups yipped in answer.

She turned back. What had she done? Anyone with any sense would have asked a thousand questions, and others, who had no sense at all, would instead introduce God to her father's cows.

But he was gone, and it would be full dark soon.

At the bottom of the tor she untied Tiny from the lone tree and rode slowly toward home, the taste of honey light still in her throat.

Now that she'd had a sit with God, Rebecca supposed she would be expected to love not just the mountains, but love the people, too. That was all he ever really wanted from his children, wasn't it? She figured she might be able to Love the World, or at least the general idea of it, if she didn't have to love people in the particular. Did she have to love the Cochrane cowboys who'd wanted to run her people off when they first arrived? What about their neighbors, the Sempels, who repulsed all Mother's efforts to be neighborly? And people were always unhappily surprising her by being just like her—scared sometimes, selfish sometimes, tired and lazy and thoughtless and uncertain.

With this in mind, Rebecca couldn't help being astonished all over again that God had allowed himself to be seen by her. She couldn't remember doing anything deserving that day, or any day in her life for that matter. She loved Mother and tried to help, but she usually felt it a sacrifice, which canceled out any credit to goodness she could have hoped for. She was, she had to admit, at times unlovely of temper, and thought a dozen unkind thoughts a day. At this very moment she could think a dozen unkind thoughts about her brother Ammon alone.

On the good side, she was fair and could see the other side of a thing. And also—well, she supposed that was all the goodness she could honestly lay claim to. She could scrub the house top to bottom, and milk a kicky cow, and quilt some, but she would rather ride her horse than do her chores, rather daydream in the hayloft than pay attention in church. She suspected she had been born more naturally wicked than others, and a lifetime of humble reflection would never make her as good as Mother and her best friend, LaRue Fletcher, already were. Considering everything, being as good as she needed to be was an appalling prospect, given her natural inclinations.

But what else could she do? It was time to reform.

Rebecca had come to her parents a daughter after six sons. Three of her brothers lived with her: Gideon, Zach, and Ammon. Another brother, William, born first, had died as a child. Two other brothers, Jared and Samuel, had chosen to stay in Utah and had families of their own.

The way Ammon told it, when Rebecca came along, she was an afterthought, a shrug, after the straight-shouldered pride of all that male offspring, a concession to God that they must take the bad with the good. But their beloved mother bent over that bit of flesh as if it were her own heart lying in the cradle, and the boys had to go along with it. When the baby girl was a year old and clearly going to live, Mother began insisting the brothers remember its name: Rebecca. Mother said it hadn't gone quite like that, but Rebecca tended to believe Ammon.

Her family's house was on the shore by Lee Creek, the barn behind the house on a rise. The house was made of logs hauled from the timber and sawn and dovetailed by hand. Father hadn't used a single nail in the building of it. It seemed more beautiful than ever to Rebecca this evening as she rode up, lamplight glowing through the sugar-sacking curtains.

She put Tiny in the barn, walked to the house, and opened the door. In her everyday voice she said, as if her heart hadn't landed on God, "I'm home."

The family was seated at the table already. Father glanced at her from under his bushy gray eyebrows, and she knew he was unhappy that she hadn't been home to help Mother with dinner.

"Late as usual," said Ammon, pushing a bowl of mashed potatoes in her direction.

Father resumed talking to his sons, as always about land and livestock and weather and their prospects as settlers. Her father and brothers got their homesteads by paying the government ten dollars and promising to prove up—building a house and working the land—in three years' time. In another year, if they could hang on, the land would be theirs. Her brothers had only rudimentary log houses on their land, which butted up against Father's, and they would continue to live at home until they got married, which couldn't happen soon enough in Rebecca's opinion.

She had never dared to think of having a homestead of her own, but now she would dare. She personally didn't know any women homesteaders, but she'd heard of a Mrs. Bedingfeld who had her own spread up Pekisko way—a widow who came to the Territories with her son and now had a ranch that rivaled even the Cochrane Ranche for profit. Rebecca had heard her referred to as a woman of character and enterprise, two adjectives Rebecca wouldn't mind having applied to herself. When she had the land for her own, she could climb the tor every day forever.

"Wolves are fat and cheeky from last winter's die-out," Gideon said, for the wolves had started up their choir again. He meant that the wolves had eaten well over the winter on the carcasses of cattle that hadn't survived the cold. Now the wolves wanted the live ones.

"Lots of new pups, and mama wolves needing to feed them," Zach said, "and our new calves look tasty. I heard the Cochrane Ranche imported wolfhounds to deal with them."

"So they did," Father said, "and the wolves dealt with the dogs most egregiously."

Rebecca thought the wild animals deserved their dinner as much as people did, but she glanced at Mother and decided not to say so. Mother expressed few opinions, whereas Rebecca had an abundance of them and rarely hesitated to bless others with them. Now she decided she would emulate her mother in all womanly virtues, and say only the most ladylike things or nothing at all.

"I don't suppose wolves will stop us," Zach said with his mouth half full. "It's the Cochrane Ranche and all their rich Eastern investors—how are we supposed to compete at the stock auction?" Eastern investors made it so Cochrane could sell his beef at lower rates than any of the other ranchers.

Father and her brothers ate in silence a few minutes, pondering, she knew, the problems that plagued them—how to keep their homesteads going, how to get through the long winter, how to get their cattle through. Pilgrim cows were not designed for the privations of the North-West Territories. In winter, they were driven by blizzards over the banks of coulees and into drifts, and splayed themselves on ice glares. In summer they were tormented by heat and flies, and broke their legs in gopher holes. They died birthing their calves as if they were delicate ladies. There was nothing buffalo about them, for they were bred to be fat and spindly-legged and tame.

It seemed a fool's dream sometimes, but to fail would mean Father and her brothers would have to return to work in the coal mines in Utah. It would be the end of their dream to have their own land, to make their living aboveground.

"We will complain less and be more grateful for the opportunity we have," Father said. "My father in England would never have dreamed of such land and such dominion for his son and my sons."

"And your daughter, Father. Someday I will have some opportunity and dominion of my own. I have found a quarter section of land I would like."

Father and her brothers stopped eating and stared at her.

"Women don't have dominion, Rebecca," Zach said. "They are part of what a man has dominion over."

"Don't you say that, Zach," she said in a rush. "I am going to have my own land, and I'm going to have dominion like nobody's business."

Her determination to say only ladylike things had lasted all of a minute, but if her father and brothers had homesteads, why shouldn't she?

"Which land is this, daughter?" Father said in a measured tone.

"The quarter section between our land and Coby's."

"That?" Ammon said. "Why would anyone want that land? It's mostly rocks and wind—even the gophers don't want to live there."

"Well I do, and I will."

Father shook his head. "Single women can't homestead, Rebecca." His voice was patient. "The law says so. You will have your own land by way of your husband when you marry."

"I will go to the land office and make inquiries," Rebecca said.

This almost constituted back talk, which was forbidden. But Mother saved the day.

"I believe I will have enough butter and eggs to sell in town in a couple of days," she said. "I shall come with you."

All heads turned to Mother.

"I am sure your father is right," she said, "but I'd like to hear what the land agent says about it. Your aunt Durden's sister-in-law homesteads in Montana—perhaps things have changed."

Rebecca was suddenly full. Blissfully full. Here was further proof that her mother was only a little lower than the angels.

Father shook his head at his plate, as if the gravy had betrayed him in some way, and said, "It's a waste of your time, Eliza, but go if you must."

After a short silence, Ammon steered the conversation back to the discussion they were having before Rebecca had interrupted. "Will we make it, Father?"

Ammon asked this—Ammon who never asked a question to which he didn't already know the answer. Ammon in all meekness was asking Father if they were going to make it. Furthermore, Father was pondering his question, as if there were no immediate and obvious answer.

"Of course we will make it!" Rebecca said. "Shame for asking, Ammon—of course we will!"

Father rested his elbows on the table and folded his hands together over his plate. "You are full of proclamations tonight, daughter. What is the source of it?"

"Because," she said.

Father seemed to consider this, and then nodded solemnly. "Always the best reason."

"The best," said Ammon.

"Because," she said, somewhat less boldly. "Because...I saw God."

Gideon choked on his food. Zach snorted. Ammon stared.

In her heart she knew that the two bore no relation, but, after all, she had seen God, and shouldn't that lend a little weight to her pronouncements?

Father looked at Rebecca the way he did when one of his

cows got the bloat. He stroked his beard, his beard which he had always had. It occurred to Rebecca for the first time that she had never in her life seen her father's entire face.

Ammon grinned wildly.

"And where did you see him, sister?" he asked.

"He was on the big rock up on the tor, looking over the flats to the mountains," Rebecca said, knowing how it must sound. She lowered her eyes. "It was a pretty sunset."

"Rebecca," Mother said, "these things are not to be trifled with."

"I'm not trifling," Rebecca said, contradicting her mother, and, for the moment, not caring.

"And what would God want by appearing to you?" Ammon asked. "Did he call you to repentance?"

"I think—I think it was an accident. Perhaps he forgot to make himself invisible."

"Forgot, eh?" Ammon said. "Let's hope he doesn't forget to make the sun come up tomorrow."

Her brothers laughed.

"Tell me," Gideon said to her, "he didn't give you a stone tablet with writing on it, did he?"

Father said, "The impertinence of seeing God at his leisure. I believe you have been afflicted with too much imagination, Rebecca, and too much time to cultivate it."

That meant he would find more work for her to do.

"The prophets saw God," Mother said quietly.

"I think, Eliza," Father said, "that we shall not compare our daughter to a prophet. Tomorrow, Rebecca, you will help me put in the potato field."

"Consider the state of your soul," Ammon intoned in

a deep voice, and Gideon and Zach shoved food in their mouths so they wouldn't laugh again.

After evening chores and family prayer, Rebecca sat on her bed and considered the state of her soul.

She was sure her mother never had an impatient thought, for she'd never seen her anything but gentle and kind, except to the odd prairie chicken. It was well-known Mother could do better with her 12-gauge shotgun than any man when a prairie chicken was needed for supper. Also Mother was a midwife, and any time of day or night, in any weather, she would go to birth a baby and stay after to help. She would clean the house, cook and carry water, and milk the cows. She did other nursing, as well, and laid out the dead, and tithed her garden and her bread to the needy, the afflicted, and the bachelor, specifically Coby Webster who lived alone, which Mother saw as a great pity. Rebecca thought it impossible for an ordinary young woman like herself to live in the shadow of such goodness.

Rebecca said her prayers lying down. She knew she should kneel, but the floor seemed so cold and hard and far away. Ammon had once told her she'd only get half the blessings she asked for if she didn't pray on her knees. Gideon said that was nonsense, but it stuck with her. So tonight she prayed for twice as much as she needed, just in case. She prayed to be kind like Mother, and pure like LaRue. She prayed, "Please bless the wolf pups so that they will eat tonight—just not our calves. And may I please have my own homestead. Two, I mean."

POTATOES

For morning chores, Rebecca must make the beds, do the breakfast dishes, milk the cow, slop the pigs, scatter some grain for the chickens, and check the nesting boxes in the darkest corner of the barn for eggs. The milking took the longest, but feeding the chickens was the worst. The chickens could tell she was the runt of the litter and always attacked her, pecking at her legs. Mother said they could smell her fear, and Rebecca said fear was the only sensible thing to feel around a chicken.

"I am not compatible with chickens, and I will not feed them anymore," she said, coming back into the house with all the eggs the chickens would allow her.

Father heard her and answered, "I am sorry to hear that, daughter, but the idler shall not eat the chicken of the laborer. Nor the eggs. Nor anything with eggs in it."

Rebecca had long understood that the best way to disappoint Father was to be afraid. Of anything. He claimed fear had been bred out of Leavitt stock generations out of mind, and she never wanted to disabuse him of this notion, even though she was afraid. She was afraid of dying in any way that would serve as a cautionary tale for generations, and she was afraid of chickens.

Rebecca sighed. "The chickens are fed every day, but your daughter has no such guarantee."

"It is good we have come to this understanding," Father said.

She replied, "When I feed them, I shall imagine them roasted."

Father and Mother had taught her the grim gospel of hard work. Every day was about survival, every thought and chore was for the single intent of holding off starvation: the cattle, the garden, the harvest, the bottling and hoarding, the milking, the churning, the haying...feeding the chickens. Cleanliness, according to her mother, was not only next to godliness, but an indication of it. Life and work were not two separate things. Work, according to her parents, was the foundation of all happiness, the very proof of faith, and the ideal way to reform a wayward soul and soften a hard heart. Rebecca worked when all was well, and she worked harder when she was in her parents' bad books.

After Rebecca had finished her chores, Father did his best to work the imagination out of her in the potato field. He ploughed the first furrow, into which she put the seed potatoes, one foot apart. When he ploughed the furrow next to it, the dirt folded over the previous row to cover the eyes.

The first few rows of potatoes had gone easily enough. Rebecca spoke cheerfully just so Father would know he had not broken her will.

"No one has claimed the quarter section between our homestead and Coby's, isn't that right, Father?" she asked.

"No, but Coby has preemption rights on it—first right of refusal."

"I shall persuade him to refuse it," she said.

"Rebecca, I have already explained to you that young ladies cannot have land until they are married to a man who does."

It was true that other than Mrs. Bedingfeld she hadn't heard of a single homestead north of the border that was owned by a woman who didn't also have a husband to go along with it. But perhaps that was only because those women hadn't the imagination for it.

"But why not, Father?"

"It's too much work for a girl. You have to prove up. You have to live and make a living on the land."

Of course, that was the hard part, she thought, living on it. But she would. If it killed her, she would live on it.

"But potatoes—that's work you can do," Father said. "So let's get this done, for I must feed you a little while yet before I can be rid of you to a husband."

After a time, the planting became tedious, and finally it was a torture. Now, having lost count of rows, her legs shook and her back was a slab of pain and her hair was wet under her bonnet and she hadn't an ounce of cheer in her.

Once they had planted their own potatoes, they must plant the charity rows. Father said she had never known true hunger, and he hoped she never would. He had, however. And that was why they planted potatoes not only for their own family but also for anyone who might need them. Her father never ate a potato, or anything else, without first being assured that his neighbors had one, too. "We all succeed or fail together," he'd said to Brother Sempel the previous fall when he'd taken a load of potatoes to them. The Sempels had no children to help with the work. This was how Rebecca knew she was in want of charity, because she dreamed only for herself, of things that had to do with no one's happiness but her own.

Still they planted and the eyes of the seed potatoes in the burlap bag began to look at her with alien pity, dropped blind into the earth. She wondered if she would ever be able to eat one of these potatoes when they grew. But then she knew she would. She was always hungry.

Rebecca entertained herself by imagining herself falling sweetly upon the ground, her hand still clutching the bag of potato eyes, and expiring with the gentlest of sighs. She would drop into a furrow, and Father would cover her body as he ploughed the next row. He would see her before the clods covered her, lovely in death, her hair and skirts fanned out charmingly. She imagined his guilt and grief as he carried her body home, and all the ways he would suffer for having worked her to death.

She stopped to rub her back.

"Work is good for the young soul," Father said.

"My soul isn't young anymore, Father. It's aged a good deal since morning."

She should long ago have given up complaining with any hope of getting anything she wanted from it. Father said the eleventh commandment was "Thou shalt not complain," but that it had been left off the stone tablets for want of room, and the world was worse for it.

At last they finished the charity rows, too, and Rebecca was surprised to find herself yet alive.

"That is a good day's work," Father said, satisfied. "We should have a good crop. In this dirt, you can plant a nail and grow a hammer."

As they walked back to the house together, Rebecca could just see the tor in the distance, and she thought how from the tor she could see Everything. Why should she not have her own land? She wanted it because she wanted it!

LAND OFFICE

Cardston was the closest town. Three years before, Brother Charles Ora Card, their ecclesiastical leader, and his band of pioneers had come by wagon train from Utah and planted their colony on Lee Creek. That first year they had created roads to the timber, built their log houses and a church, and now the settlement boasted a butcher shop, a store with dry goods, and other businesses, along with plans for a cheese factory and a piggery. They had named their town Cardston in honor of Brother Card, and that was where Rebecca and her mother were headed that morning.

"Father says even the queen of England doesn't have what we have here in the Territories," Rebecca said. Her parents had moved from England just after they were married.

Mother replied, "On the other hand, the queen mightn't want it, given how cold it gets."

"I don't mind the cold," Rebecca said. It was almost true—each winter she felt her blood braving up to the cold, changing its recipe so she'd be able to bear it.

The sky here wasn't gently gray and softly wet, the way Mother said it was in England. Here it was vast and relentless—it had colored moons and moonbows, sun dogs, and lightning storms like the end of the earth. But the sky today was a benevolent blue.

After Mother traded her butter and eggs for sugar, she walked with Rebecca to the land agent's office. The agent was Mr. Caldwell, who was not a member of their faith. He had brown teeth, for he was a prodigious tobacco chewer, as was evident by the tobacco stains surrounding the spittoon. The flesh on the inside of his mouth was black. He stood behind a high counter, and behind him was the venerated image of Queen Victoria of England and Empire.

Rebecca took a deep breath and held out her hand. "Good day. I am Rebecca Leavitt and this is my mother, Mrs. Elizabeth Leavitt."

"I know your husband," Mr. Caldwell said to Mother. "Do you come on his errand?"

"No, I come for myself," Rebecca said. "I wish to be a homesteader as soon as I've raised my ten-dollar fee. I would like the quarter section of land between my father's spread and Coby Webster's. Father says I can't, and I've come to prove I can."

She felt stronger now that she'd out with it, bigger, taller even than Mr. Caldwell, and she wondered if she'd grown just by virtue of saying those words.

The agent spit and missed the spittoon.

"Miss," he said, "you are a girl."

"A woman," she said. "Eighteen soon. The age you need to be to homestead."

He folded his hands over the counter and smiled brownly.

"Miss, your father is right. Single women in the Territories are not allowed to homestead."

Rebecca had to let that settle a moment. Of course Father was right.

She raised her eyes to the portrait of Queen Victoria, formidable in lace and satin and a baby crown upon her head, and lowered her eyes again to the land agent. She dared not speak.

"I'm curious, Mr. Caldwell," Mother said, "I have a relative in Montana who has her own homestead—"

"Yes, but in the Dominion of Canada," said the agent, "the only way for a woman to get a homestead is if she is the head of a household, meaning she is a widow with children."

"But how is this fair?" Rebecca asked. She glanced at Mother and remembered to modulate her voice. "How can this be right?"

"It needn't be fair or right, miss, because it is the law. There's a difference between what is right and what is legal, and fair doesn't enter into things at all. Under the law, a woman is a person in matters of pains and penalties, but not in matters of rights and privileges."

"Are you saying, Mr. Caldwell," Rebecca said, "that by law I cannot homestead because I am not a person?"

"That's about the sum of it." He turned to Mother. "If a big ol' buffalo wandered by with ten dollars pinned to her horns, I couldn't sell her that land now, could I."

"But you could if it was a big ol' male buffalo?" Rebecca said.

He frowned. "Sooner a male buffalo than a cheeky girl," he said.

Rebecca studied the counter between her and the land agent. She was pretty sure she could leap over it and take him down. But this counter—it had the whole government and even the Mounties behind it. A counter like that was not to be leaped over or contradicted. And Mother, of course, would surely perish of shame.

"Mr. Caldwell," said Mother, "what if my husband were to purchase the land and put Rebecca's name on the deed?"

"He could do that, but he'd have to pay outright, of course. One hundred and sixty acres at three dollars an acre."

"But that's—that's four hundred eighty dollars!" Rebecca said.

"It is, and a bargain at that. Besides," Mr. Caldwell said, "Coby Webster has preemption rights on that piece of land. Also, Pietr Sempel has shown interest in case Webster don't want it. And you know, that land has water access so no matter who wants it, the Cochrane outfit will make a stink about someone living there and putting up fences."

Rebecca knew her family didn't have that kind of money, and never had. Everything they owned they had built or bartered for.

Mother tipped her head regally, and Rebecca knew what that meant. It meant to behave like a lady no matter what.

Rebecca looked up again at the picture of the queen.

"Is the queen a person?" she asked.

"Queen is different," said Mr. Caldwell.

"How so?"

"She's got a crown, don't she."

The thing was, Rebecca thought, when you set out to Love the World, you had to love land agents who grinned at you brownly and were happy at your sorrows. You had to imagine that God was his Papa, too. But no, she hadn't been afflicted with that much imagination.

"I thank you for your time," Rebecca said, but she didn't mean it.

"My pleasure, miss," he said, running his hands over the countertop.

She and Mother left.

On the way home, they were silent for a time.

Ducks flew out of a swale, their wings making a soft thunder. The pulsing prairie arched its back, half woke up as it stretched along toward the mountains, then sank and sighed into the deep green timber to the west. From there the mountains rose up blue and white without a by-your-leave. Nobody could love it all more than she did. Even the weather—when it had snowed in July, and was warm as spring on Christmas Day, she'd loved the land all the more for having its own mind about things.

Well, if she wouldn't be allowed to homestead, she'd just have to buy it outright! It would be better to buy the land outright anyway. That way she wouldn't have to prove up, build a house and fences and a barn and a corral and a pigpen. She needn't spoil the land at all! She could let it be! Of course, at three dollars an acre, that would be a very great deal of money...

Suddenly Mother stopped the wagon. Without a word, she took her 12-guage shotgun from the wagon box where it always lived. She shot into the prairie, got out of the wagon, and returned with a fat prairie chicken.

"We'll have this tomorrow," she said, getting back in the wagon. As they started off again she said, "So it is just as your father told us."

"I shall have to earn four hundred eighty dollars, Mother," Rebecca said. "I will stand on my own land, and nobody will move me. It will be my land right down to the center of the earth, and all the way up to heaven. A bird flying over my land will be my bird. A gopher on my land can live and keep its tail. Nobody will boss me on my land, and I'll go up to the Sitting Rock every day as long as I live."

"The sitting rock?"

"On the tor."

Mother nodded thoughtfully. "Well," she said after a moment, "a daughter might have what a woman cannot."

Supper was sugar-baked beans and day-old bread, and after the men had eaten almost all, Mother said to Father, "We talked to Mr. Caldwell about the problem of Rebecca's land. It is true that a single woman in the Dominion of Canada cannot homestead. But Mr. Caldwell told us you could buy the land under your name and put her name on the deed as well."

Father looked around at his sons as if to confirm what he was hearing.

"Buy the land? Outright? Do you know how much money that would be?"

"I do," Mother said. "It is a great deal of money. She will have to earn the money herself, of course."

"Yes! She will!" Rebecca said.

Father and her brothers looked at Rebecca and at each other and then at Mother.

Rebecca was thinking, if she could get a chicken of her own and sell the eggs... If she could get more milk out of the milch cow, she could sell the extra butter... She could make bonnets to sell—Mother had taught her... Of course, none of it would come even close to making that kind of money.

"Well," Father said. "Certainly. If she can earn the money and convince Coby not to exercise his preemption rights in the meantime, well, I guess I could do that for her."

Mother tipped her head elegantly, and began clearing away dishes.

"And if I own the land outright," Rebecca said, "I don't have to prove up. I can leave the land as pretty as it is now."

"You mean, not work the land?" Ammon said.

"That is what I mean."

Father said, as if it didn't matter anyway for she would never have the land, "You can't live on scenery."

Ammon said, "If you find a way to earn that much money, I hope you'll let me know, sister."

Rebecca said she would, and Mother changed the subject.

That night, Mother came into her room holding her pretty enameled box, shiny black with dainty white and pink flowers painted on it. Mother said it was from Japan. In it she kept baby teeth and wisps of baby hair tied with blue ribbons, and one with a pink ribbon. It sat on a shelf in the sitting room, shaming all around it that was earthy and homespun.

She handed the box to Rebecca. "You have it now, for your savings. For your land."

Rebecca held the box in her hands.

"Shall I brush out your hair Rebecca?"

Hair brushing was a way Mother reminded Rebecca that they were special to each other, being the only women in a houseful of men whose noise and hunger and tempers took up so much of their day.

For your land, Mother had said. And Mother never lied.

THE DANCE

Rebecca felt impatient every time she looked at her empty money box, but it lifted her spirits to know that there was going to be a dance at the church. Everyone would come, young and old, and dance until the wee hours of the morning.

That Friday, after the housework was done, Rebecca helped Mother prepare food for the midnight lunch at the dance, including frying doughnuts. At last it was time to get ready. Rebecca was so happy to be seeing her friend LaRue that she rushed her bath and accidentally used too much vinegar rinse in her hair. When she came out in her church dress, Mother said affectionately, "It's bordering on immodest, all those curls of yours."

"I don't do it on purpose," Rebecca said.

"You both look very nice," Father said.

"Does she have to look like that?" Ammon said grumpily in Rebecca's direction.

"Nothing can be done," Mother said cheerfully. "It is your duty to be proud of such a sister."

"Pride is a canker," Ammon said.

"You know what I mean, Ammon," Mother said.

"Well, I am proud."

"Ammon, do you mean it?" Rebecca asked.

"Don't go making more of it than it is," he replied. "Anyway, you smell like a pickle."

In the wagon on the way to Cardston, Rebecca studied Ammon. He was a perfect gentleman to everyone, or so everyone liked to tell her. People admired him for being the first to help a needing family with the haying or a barn raising, and for having most of the hymns memorized. But Rebecca wished his admirers could see how he loved to tease her at home.

Mother said her brothers were handsome as Greek statues, but, in Rebecca's opinion, that didn't say much for Greeks or for statues. Her brothers were serviceable enough, she supposed, as far as men went. All the girls admired them. She thought how nice it would be, now they had their own homesteads and their own log houses, if they would find wives to help shoulder the work of cleaning up after them.

Mother had said not long ago that her sons' houses looked sad and empty-eyed without mistresses to add their touch, and Father joked that Gideon and Zach were so old they were practically in breach of their obligation to marry. Mother said there was no such obligation, other than to one's own happiness, and Father agreed.

Rebecca wondered deeply about marriage, now that she was of marriageable age herself. Her parents seemed to enjoy so blessed a state as to be holy, though Rebecca thought it might have required Christian forbearance and some hefting of one's cross to get to that blissful state. Rebecca wanted a husband who would love her the way Father loved Mother: like Adam loved Eve, as if she were the only woman on earth. She and her husband would wake up in the same bed and live in the same house and look out the same windows and eat the same dinner. They would love each other's children and each other's land, and one would be there when the other died... She frowned. She could always imagine the saddest ending to the happiest story.

All the girls her age spoke as though marriage was the end of all being, the pinnacle of feminine achievement, but Rebecca had more than once wondered, in spite of her parents' happiness, what one did for excitement for the rest of one's life once the wedding was over. Babies of course, but they could be deadly. She had once met a spinster who seemed decidedly happy—trim, well-dressed, not at all looking as if she were only half of a whole, but rather quite whole all on her own. Still, Rebecca had high hopes for romance, and the lofty example of her parents to live up to.

Mother said, "Are you excited about the dance, Rebecca?"

"I'm looking forward to seeing LaRue."

"I mean the dance itself. It's different, now that you're older."

"Why, Mother?"

"What is a dance for, but to consider husbands?"

"Then for what reason do married people come to the dance?"

"Why, to make sure you consider the right husbands," Mother said.

When they pulled up outside the church, light glowed through the windows and the open door. Men and women greeted her family in a variety of accents – English, Scottish, Swedish, and some Rebecca didn't know. But their children, running about the yard laughing, were growing new voices, a new language, their vowels stretched flat by this prairie land. Father and her brothers went to spread sawdust on the floor to get it good and slidey for the minuets and schottisches. Mother, with the help of friends, carried her food inside.

Though the Cochrane cowboys were resentful of these fence-building settlers, they sometimes showed up to their dances. Father said they got little in the way of entertainment at the ranch, and still less the company of women, never mind their cooking, so no one would send them away, even though there was an uneasy peace between their people and the cowboys.

She had been told that just after the first families of the colony arrived at Lee Creek, the foreman of the Cochrane Ranche and some of his cowboys had lined their horses up on a rise and watched with unfriendly eyes as the settlers ploughed a communal garden.

"Should we run 'em off, boss?" one cowboy had asked.

"Leave 'em be," he said. "They'll winter-kill."

Her people hadn't winter-killed — not yet — though winter had done its best to buck them off.

The cowboys were having a tense conversation with Levi Howard, who was holding a horse by the lead.

"That's one of ours for sure," said one of the Cochrane cowboys, nodding in the direction of the horse.

"I found it in my south field," Levi said. "You know as well as I that the law says a horse has to be branded before it's a year old, and this one's at least two. That means it's for the finding." Rebecca thought that Levi, as the owner of a horse ranch, should know.

"We didn't have to worry about branding so quick before you folks came along," another cowboy said.

"Guess you boys will have to fight me for it," Levi said. "One at a time, of course."

Rebecca thought that was a brave stance, and wasn't unhappy to think about one of those cowboys getting a sore nose.

Suddenly Coby Webster was there, with his low, easy voice and his friendly way.

"You came to dance, didn't you, gents?" he said to the cowboys. "You don't want to cause trouble, I guess."

"We came for the dancing," said one, "and then we just got to saying how that horse looks like one of our breeds."

"And I was just saying a maverick is a maverick," Levi replied. "You get slipshod about branding your horseflesh, you lose it."

"True enough," Coby said, "but how about we stretch the law for the sake of being good neighbors?" He said it low and slow to the evening sky, as if it were just something to be considered.

Levi considered. Then he took the lead off the horse, slapped its rump, and shook his head as one of the cowboys grabbed it. "I've got better horses than this one anyway," he said with a wry smile.

Coby nodded and said to the cowboys, "There's no strong drink at our dances, gents, as you know. This party is as dry as a buffalo skull in drought."

"We know that."

"Then you're welcome to join us," Coby said, gesturing to the door.

The cowboys entered the meetinghouse.

Coby turned to Levi.

"I could have taken them," Levi said.

"Yes," Coby said, "and I would have helped."

Levi placed a hand on Coby's shoulder and they smiled at each other. Then Levi tipped his hat to Rebecca as if she were a lady, and went into the dance.

"Coming, Reb?" Coby asked, using his childhood name for her.

She nodded and followed them in.

Coby's family had lived near hers in Utah. Coby was three years older than Rebecca and had, just like her brothers, worked in the coal mines from the age of twelve. A little over two years ago, when he'd heard the Leavitts were going north to the Territories, Coby asked if he could travel with them.

Coby was always around the Leavitts' house as he was friends with Rebecca's brothers, and, she supposed, with her too. But her feelings about him changed shortly before they left for the north. They'd been at the wedding of her oldest brother, and Rebecca had romance on her mind. Casually she said to Coby, "What makes a boy like a girl? Mother says it's charity and good works, and I've all but given up on ever acquiring those virtues."

"It helps to be pretty," Coby answered.

"Am I pretty?" she asked him.

"Prettiest by far, though a bit spoiled."

"And you say this right in front of me, Coby?"

"Generally you take the truth well."

"The truth is a grand thing, except when it comes to oneself," she said.

He had nothing to say about that, but quick as a bird, he leaned over and kissed her on the cheek.

Just then Ammon had come up behind them.

"I saw you kiss!" he said, pointing, and then he walked away grinning.

Rebecca was aghast.

"Coby Webster, you take that back!" she said.

"Never will," he said, walking after Ammon.

"I'll—I'll tell the bishop!"

She forgave Coby after a few days, though their friendship wasn't quite the same after that. She hadn't made any particular effort to forgive Ammon.

Inside the church, Brother Archibald and his band were warming up, and everyone was talking and joking together. Rebecca looked for Levi among the crowd, without appearing to look for him. She was impressed that Levi had been willing to fight the cowboys, impressed that he would walk away from a fight. She hoped he would ask her to dance — she would ask him about his fine horses. Coby preferred Blackfoot ponies, and kept some on his land. A pony, she noted, could never be as lovely a thing as a fine horse.

Levi was a remittance man, the third son of a titled Englishman. All his father's estate would go to the first son, under the rule of primogeniture, so Levi had been given money to go far away from England. Loving horses, he had come west to the Territories to establish a horse ranch and practice his faith. He still had some of his English accent, which Rebecca liked.

Rebecca could see Levi now. He and her brothers and Coby, along with some of the other young men of marriage-able age, were surrounded by admiring girls, the prettiest among them Radonna Beck.

Rebecca's envy of Radonna was all the proof she needed of her own hard heart. But how could she help it, looking at Radonna in her resplendent pink dress, and Rebecca dressed in serviceable brown? Radonna was pampered at home by her mother, who saw in her daughter's beauty an obligation on the part of the world to treat her like a porce-lain doll. Radonna, according to others, had fine manners. She could quote scripture and do fancy cooking and was an admired quilter. In short, she was everything Rebecca was not, including an accomplished flirt. Zach, Gideon, and Coby didn't seem much taken in by all her flirting, but Ammon and Levi were soaking it up.

LaRue came, late as always, for she had to help her younger brothers get washed and combed and ushered into the wagon. It seemed LaRue's mother was the caretaker of the youngest, and LaRue the caretaker of the rest as they moved up the line, and maybe it was all that mothering that made her the good soul she was.

LaRue's heart was a jewelry box—it sang when you opened it. It was velvet-lined and soft, yet it clamped down on treasures—anything Rebecca told her was safe. A slen-der thing, and half a head shorter than Rebecca, LaRue was the loveliest creature Rebecca had ever seen. Some girls' faces bragged about their beauty—Radonna's, for example. But you had to take a little time to discover LaRue's beauty. It was like that with each of LaRue's perfections. You had to know her for years to realize you'd never heard her say an unkind word about anyone, not even about Sister Yardley's singing. Even Brother Card snickered about Sister Yardley's singing. You had to watch her closely to see her small, quiet kindnesses to anyone who came near. LaRue remembered everything about people—How are your rosebushes faring, Sister Shuling? she would ask. Have you finished bordering your star quilt, Sister Doxie? Is your cousin's health any better, Sister Downing? LaRue lived soft on the world, always adding to the happiness of others, whereas Rebecca tromped around with her mind mostly made up about things. Rebecca never listened when people told her about their roses and quilts and cousins, and if she accidentally did listen, she promptly forgot. How did somebody else's roses matter in the grand plan? But LaRue understood the mattering of small things.

The two girls were the precise opposite of each other in every other way, as well. Rebecca was the youngest after six brothers, and LaRue the oldest before six brothers. LaRue already had the responsibilities of a grown woman, whereas Rebecca was allowed to wander.

Rebecca had no idea why LaRue persisted in being her friend, but until LaRue figured out that she was unworthy of her, Rebecca would cling to her and be grateful for the gift of her.

She rushed to LaRue and embraced her.

"Look at Ammon and the girls," Rebecca said.

"I'm not surprised they like him," LaRue said.

"LaRue," Rebecca said, "what do you mean? Ammon has a hard heart."

"I think others see your brother a little differently, perhaps, than you do, Rebecca. You know your brothers are always the first to arrive when help is needed, and the last to go. When Brother Timms broke his leg, he said your brothers cared for his farm so well he considered breaking the other leg."

"That is only proof they can do their duty," Rebecca said.

"Ammon is very handsome."

"He is?"

"Very. And gallant."

"Gallant! He just told me I smelled like a pickle."

"And kind."

"Kind? Stop. I can't bear it."

"But don't you love your brother, Rebecca?"

"I do, but against all reason."

"I've always liked him, you know..."

"You like everybody," Rebecca said. "LaRue, you must not marry any of my brothers, for as long as you have one hand and one foot, they will expect you to cook and wait upon them hand and foot."

LaRue smiled dreamily and stared at Ammon across the room.

Rebecca couldn't figure out why LaRue would settle for her brother when it was obvious that she should marry an apostle. Of course, there weren't many of those, and not a one in the North-West Territories that she knew of. Besides, you had to find and marry an apostle when he was still young, and long before he became an apostle, and apostleship could be hard to predict. Sometimes you couldn't tell apostle material until their hair turned white and their faces got sad from feeling the sorrows of others over a long period of time.

"Don't worry, Rebecca," La Rue said, patting her arm. "Ammon would never notice a mouse like me."

"A mouse? Why you're the best girl in the land — probably in the Dominion of Canada."

"You're the only one who thinks so."

"Well, if Ammon doesn't think so, it would only prove my opinion of him."

The music began, and a few married couples made a square.

Rebecca said, "LaRue, I am going to have my own land."

"I beg pardon."

"I'm going to have my own land."

LaRue stared. "Can you without a husband?"

Rebecca shrugged. "I mean to own it myself without a man."

LaRue looked astounded. "But—what will you do with land that comes without a husband?"

"I shall sit on it. And observe sunsets."

She wanted to tell LaRue about her sit with God, but after her family's reaction she felt shy of it.

"All I have to do is raise a little money."

Brother Archibald and his band started to play in earnest, and Loyal and Kit, two young men in their group, normally so quiet and stoic, began dancing wildly around the room together. Soon many were dancing, except for the Cochrane cowboys who stood along the wall, holding it up with all their might, their eyes full of the lantern light and the girls. The girls thought themselves too virtuous to dance with a gentile cowboy, so they hadn't flirted with them the way they had with the other men.

Suddenly LaRue left Rebecca's side and walked straight up to one of the cowboys. She smiled and said, "Wouldn't you like to ask me to dance?"

Without a word he shoved his hat at his friend and led LaRue onto the dance floor.

After that, the cowboys got up the courage to ask other girls to dance and they said yes. Rebecca marveled at her friend who always knew the right thing to do, even when the right thing seemed the wrong thing.

Father and Gideon and Zach each asked Rebecca to dance. Ammon was busy asking many girls to dance, even the shyer ones, and even some of the matrons. He offered his arm to take them to the dance floor, and talked and laughed with them, and appeared to be gallant indeed.

"What a fine young man your brother Ammon is, Rebecca," said old Mother Laidlaw. "He is the embodiment of virtue, I'm sure."

Rebecca followed her adoring eyes to be sure she was indeed talking about Ammon.

"Not my brother, ma'am," Rebecca said to her. "He is not the embodiment. I can vouch for that."

"Now, now, Rebecca. I can understand that you'd feel badly, living in his shadow as you must feel you do. But let's not allow envy to blind our eyes to the good in others."

Mother Laidlaw said all this without removing her admiring eyes from Ammon.

Rebecca resisted the urge to put her finger in one of those adoring eyes. Live in Ammon's shadow? Why she did no such thing!

On the other side of it, well, maybe she did.

Ammon was ever polite and helpful, faithful and respectful of his elders. He only teased his sister, she supposed. Nobody besides Rebecca would be surprised that LaRue had chosen him.

When Ammon wandered close by, Rebecca said to him, nodding toward LaRue on the dance floor, "LaRue likes you best, you know."

"Oh?"

"It's her only flaw."

Gideon came to stand next to Rebecca, silent, as he was often silent. He seemed never to fit in the confines of church, even when people were dancing in it. He had shoulders like an ox and a broad back and thick arms and thighs. He worked methodically, but relentlessly. He started out the day at a slow, steady pace, but at the end of the day, when everyone else was spent, he was still going at the same pace. When he and his brothers chopped wood, his brothers chopped quickly and soon had a good pile and were worn out. Gideon's stack, however, was always the highest by the time he was done, because he just kept on. But Gideon had two weaknesses: Philemon Charles, and an inability to form complete sentences around Philemon Charles.

Philemon, on the other hand, talked as if the air was not

quite breathable without words floating in it. After a visit from Philemon, words could be found for days in cups and corners and teaspoons and thimbles. She asked questions of others until they, too, were chatting like a tree full of birds on a spring day. A soul couldn't be lonely if she lived within a mile of Philemon.

"I'm going to ask her to dance," Gideon told Rebecca.

"You should."

"I will," he said.

"Will you?"

"No," he said.

"Yes," she said, "or I shall have to tease you mercilessly."

Gideon left her to approach Philemon. He hovered about and cast a mournful look at Rebecca, who nodded vigorously.

Speak, she thought, speak, Gideon. He seemed to gather his courage and said, "Philemon —" Then nothing.

Finally he held out his hand and led Philemon onto the dance floor. And they both seemed pleased. Philemon chatted enough for the both of them. Rebecca was asked to dance a quadrille with Loyal, a schottische with Kit, and a polka with Vern. It seemed she was going to be asked to dance by everyone but Levi, the very one she hoped to dance with. She noted that he had danced with Radonna twice.

The dance was well underway when Kootenai Brown entered the church to the hurrahs of everyone. The men gathered round to shake his hand and clap his shoulder. He was a short man with a long mustache, and Rebecca liked his Irish way of speaking.

Kootenai had been living with his family in the

mountains before Rebecca's people had come. He knew the mountains and rivers and wildlife better than anyone. If you could get him talking, he had the best stories.

"How is the fishing these days?" one of the men asked, and Kootenai told of a fifty-pound lake trout he'd caught a few days back.

The men shook their heads and laughed. He didn't seem to mind, and Rebecca decided that was because it was probably true. People possessed of a true story, she'd learned, didn't mind so much when nobody believed them.

Rebecca listened as the conversation turned to irrigation. Her people had come to the Territories with irrigation skills. But federal officials didn't want any talk of irrigation for fear it would spook potential settlers who wouldn't want to live on arid land that needed irrigating.

"I hear Card is in conversation with Charles Magrath about digging a canal," said Kootenai.

Businessman Elliott Glat and his assistant and land commissioner Charles Magrath had a vision of settling the Canadian west. Magrath knew Rebecca's people had the know-how for digging the canal, having irrigated the deserts of Utah, but people not of their faith in surrounding communities protested. They feared losing political control if more of her people immigrated to provide the skills and labor for building the canal.

"We've been down that road," someone said, "and it never works out. They'll never let us build it."

Across the way, Rebecca saw Ammon ask LaRue to dance. LaRue's face never blushed, but her neck could go three shades of pink when she was flustered. Rebecca watched as her neck made its way through all three shades and invented a fourth. She wondered how God could make her friend so perfect and leave her with so little judgment about men. LaRue thought all the marriageable young men had their good points. When the girls whispered together about which of them they would never marry, LaRue had something to say in defense of each one.

After their dance, Ammon deposited LaRue beside Rebecca casually, as if he had no idea he'd been dancing with the best girl in the Territories. Zach joined them, too.

"Zach, you should dance," Rebecca said.

"What if there's only one girl for you and she's not here?" he said.

Rebecca scanned the gathering—it seemed that just about everyone was there. Not Florence Andreeson, who never made an effort to display her charms at dances and the like. But it couldn't be Florence. Florence, it was well-known, was a proponent of suffrage, and Rebecca thought Zach was too fond of the patriarchal order, too sensitive to his responsibilities as a man, to take an interest in Florence. She wondered what sort of girl he would choose, and why she wasn't there. Perhaps he had met a girl in Lethbridge when he'd gone to the stock auction.

She also wondered, looking at the assembled congregation, how they could call themselves saints, Latter-day or otherwise, for they were a pretty ordinary lot. That brother dancing a jig like a wooden puppet, that woman with a laugh like a donkey, all those girls mooning about like they'd never seen a boy before and almost fainting when Levi or Ammon asked one of them to dance. She wished dearly that they'd not try her charitable feelings—or at least, the charitable feelings she hoped to have one day. She wondered if it would be all right if she could Love the World by telling everyone how they could stop annoying her...

The more Levi didn't ask her to dance, the more annoyed she became. She was just about to complain to LaRue about it when Levi appeared before her and asked her to dance.

They danced a square dance, and Rebecca saw Radonna frowning at her and Levi. After the square, the music changed.

"I requested this song just for you," Levi said.

Rebecca could hardly believe he was going to dance another dance with her!

He took her left hand and placed it on his shoulder. He took her right hand with his left, wrapped his other hand around her waist. She could feel the warmth of his hand through her dress.

"One slow step," he said to her so only she could hear, "and two quick steps." He counted, and she followed easily.

Everyone stared.

"It's called the waltz, ladies and gents!" Levi called.

Rebecca had heard of the waltz, but it was considered risqué. She admired Levi for shocking the older ladies, and she had to admit she liked being the center of attention. But most of all she liked being guided by his warm hand on her waist. A few other young couples started to waltz as well, clumsily at first, but soon they, too, were gliding gracefully about the room. Rebecca felt as if she were flying— she felt brave and a little wicked all at once. They glided by Radonna, who glared at her. When the dance was over, Levi said she did brilliantly and left her by the wall with a smile and a nod. She found she needed to lean ever so slightly against that wall.

And then Coby asked her to dance. He led her in a square dance, very proper, concentrating on the right steps. Her brothers admired Coby for his strength and skill as a rancher, and for running his spread alone as he did, without someone to cook for him. Rebecca had said that he was often enough at their table for Sunday dinner, and Mother said it was because that boy was "the workingest boy God ever framed from the dust."

He seemed just an ordinary young man to Rebecca. Quiet. Tall. A bouncy Adam's apple. He did have long eyelashes, but they were a waste on a man after all.

As he led her in the dance, respectfully, careful of the steps, Rebecca couldn't help wishing for another thrilling waltz. When the dance was over, Coby took her back to the bit of wall where he'd found her.

She decided now was the perfect time for her to ask.

"Coby, you know that quarter section of land just north of your property, between Father's property and yours?"

"I know it," he said.

"The land agent said you have preemption rights on it."

"I do."

"So are you going to exercise your rights?"

"I haven't decided yet."

"Somebody wants it."

"Yes, I know," he said. "Sempel has been pressuring me."

"I mean, I want it. I want that land for myself."

He looked confused. "You mean your father . . . ?" he said.

"No. I mean me. Myself."

His Adam's apple made a particularly impressive bounce. "You? Gosh sakes, Rebecca."

"Don't swear. And please not to remind me that I'm a girl. If you will give up your right to buy it first, Father will buy it in his name and add me to the deed. All I have to do is earn the money to pay for it outright, since women aren't persons and aren't allowed to homestead."

Coby looked as if he was doing sums in his head.

"What I'm asking is, if you decide you don't want it, could you hold on to your rights until I've earned the money—keep it out of the hands of Brother Sempel until then?"

"You've got it all worked out," he said.

"Yes. Well . . . all but how to get the money. When does your right expire, Coby?"

"End of next year."

"Then I'll do it. I have to have it, Coby, so I can just sit on the tor and stare at those mountains till I'm full of them."

His Adam's apple bounced from the bottom of his throat to the top and back down to the bottom. His eyes were particularly beautiful, she thought, when they were worried— was he worried? Why would he be worried?

He looked at her with his eyelashy eyes and said, "How will you get the money?"

"Coby," she said, "have you ever had a miracle?"

"No," he said. "Can't say as I have. But I would like a miracle. Just one. Something to hold on to on a bitter day."

"Well, I have had one, so I know they're out there."

"Well then," he said, "when you have the money, come to me. If I decide I don't want it, the three of us can go to the land office together, and you can buy the land the minute I relinquish my rights."

Rebecca was certain that Coby wouldn't want the land, and in her mind, the matter was settled.

Coby looked like he might say something more, but just then Joe Cosley arrived: mountain man, gentile, fabled trapper, and fancy shooter. He liked his drink, but he liked his nondrinking neighbors, too.

"How's that girl of yours in Montana, Joe?" someone called out to him.

"Well, gents, I'm going to be engaged!"

Rebecca stood on her toes to see Joe fish in his pocket and pull out a ring with a bit of starlight stuck on it. The women close by gasped.

"A diamond," one said.

Rebecca had heard of diamond rings, of course, but she had never laid eyes on one, even from a distance, until now.

"This diamond comes all the way from New York City," Joe said. "Cost me two thousand dollars. It's for my girl, Elizabeth, if she'll marry me."

Rebecca said to Coby she had not known Joe was rich, though she knew he was the best trapper in the territory.

"They say he can do a seventy-mile trap run in a single day," Coby said. "If he does even half that, it's an amazement."

The girls must each look at the ring, wishing it could be theirs, glancing at Joe Cosley as if to remind themselves that such a ring would necessarily come with him as a husband.

Coby went to get something to eat and the band started up

again, and everyone danced and mostly behaved themselves. Joe Cosley danced with his hat on, his fancy hat with the embroidered flowers under the brim. He wouldn't dance with anyone more than once, out of loyalty to his girl in Montana.

The Mounties came from Fort Macleod in their scarlet jackets with polished buttons. One of them was paying particular attention to Philemon, which made Gideon look wretched. But Radonna was the belle of the ball. It was good the Mounties were there, or she may have inspired a fistfight among the Cochrane cowboys. When Levi saw that he had competition in both cowboys and Mounties, he gave Radonna more of his attentions, and she in turn showed her preference for him.

"She likes him," Coby said, handing Rebecca a cookie.

"Who?"

"Radonna. She likes Levi."

"She makes that clear," Rebecca said. "Coby, do you believe couples who marry were destined to be together?"

"No, I can't say I do."

"Why not?" she asked. "God has planned everything out so well, why would he leave the most important thing to chance?"

He rubbed his chin. "Well, but wouldn't it be worse to think you had no say over the most important thing?"

She thought about that while she finished her cookie. It was true that she loved her say.

She was still thinking about it when another waltz began, and Levi asked her to dance again.

She had other questions she would have liked to discuss with Coby, she thought, as Levi led her around the dance floor. Was it good for Levi to defend his right to the maverick? Or good for Coby to make the peace? Was it virtue for the girls to avoid the cowboys? Or for LaRue to dance with them and make everyone realize they were nice boys after all? Was it unseemly of her to waltz with Levi, when she knew the true unseemliness was her satisfaction at seeing Radonna frown at them waltzing? She decided that a dance was no place to work out her salvation.

The dance went on until the wee hours, and at last it was time to clean up and go home.

Rebecca hated cleaning up, but Radonna was among the first to pitch in and Rebecca wouldn't be outdone. She was washing up dishes from the midnight lunch when Radonna, with two of her friends, came to dry.

"Levi is a bold thing, isn't he, Rebecca," Radonna said. "Waltzing. Of course, I wouldn't."

"No. You wouldn't," Rebecca said.

"He danced with you more than anyone, Radonna," said one of the other girls.

"Yes," Radonna said. "He did, didn't he. But...not a waltz." She put down the tea towel. "Come, girls, I think we're needed elsewhere."

Never mind.

She had talked and laughed with LaRue. Coby had said he'd hold on to his preemption rights until she could buy the land. And she had the memory of waltzing with Levi. The dance, she decided, had been a success.

CHURCH

Spring and summer meant never having to miss church, and so they never missed. Her people came from nearby homesteads to pray and sing and admonish one another in the word of the Lord. They had benches now to sit on — seating at first had been spring seats from wagons, nail kegs, and bags of oats. Everyone was very proud of those hard benches.

They gathered in the yard, talking and laughing and shaking hands; the children running about before they must endure the torture of sitting still for an hour or more; the girls flirting with the young men, and the young men flirting back; the women taking attendance of the heart, knowing the secret burdens that women carry, offering quiet love to the widow, the sister newly arrived and missing her family, the woman expecting her fifth child, the mother whose daughter had just moved away to marry.

Rebecca wanted to talk to Levi, but decided she would take her example from Mother and LaRue and visit with the sisters who might need a word of kindness. She chose the most frightening of all — Sister Gladden — who had a palsy that caused her unceasingly to shake her head. She was a dauntless pioneer who had crossed the plains to Utah and now had come north with her son and all her wealth to support the new settlement. Rebecca had never spoken to her before. She had always suspected the older woman shook her head because she was in a continual state of disappointment or disapproval at the rest of them for not equalling her standard of good works.

"Good morning, Sister Gladden," Rebecca said bravely. "How are you today?"

"You're Eliza Leavitt's girl," she said.

"Yes, ma'am."

"I hope you are a good young lady, because your mother deserves it."

"I am not good yet," Rebecca said, "but I have time."

"You don't want to be like me and have God make you always to shake your head at your own sins," Sister Gladden said with a smile.

"But you are astonishingly sinless!" she replied.

Sister Gladden chuckled and patted her cheek. "If you don't make your mother proud, you will at least make her laugh."

Rebecca saw Mother calling out to Sister Sempel, who stopped, reluctantly it seemed, to speak to her. Sister Sempel always looked like she hadn't had enough sleep the night before.

"We're having a quilting bee at Thornsbys' on Wednesday. Shall you and I go together?"

"Oh, I don't know," Sister Sempel said. She glanced toward her husband, who was approaching.

"Let's go, Lois," he said.

"I was just inviting your wife to come with me to the quilting bee...," Mother said.

"Don't know how she's got time for that nonsense. Just a roomful of women gossiping anyway. Now we'll be on our way."

Sister Sempel followed him, and Mother stood watching after her. Then she turned to go into church.

Rebecca looked for Father to tell him she needn't go to church now, for in discovering how wrong she had been about Sister Gladden's true nature, she had already had a sermon in how not to judge others. She found him around back of the building taking a cigarette out of his pocket.

"Right on the church grounds, Father?" she said. It was well-known that Father smoked out in the Vicary field, where he often walked when he had things to work out in his mind. Mother couldn't see that field from any window in their house. But Rebecca had never seen him smoke at the church.

"You'd best not do that in front of me, Father. Mother wouldn't like it."

"Then you'd best get into the chapel," Father said. He lit the match on his boot, and got started.

"Father, why do you smoke when the Church and Mother say not to?"

"That is an important question, daughter," he said. He breathed in the smoke as if it were sweet spring air.

She waited, but he didn't go on.

"And is there an answer?" she asked.

"Surely there is one."

"And will you tell it to me?"

"No, for I do not know it."

She thought about that for a moment. "Does Mother know the answer?"

"Mother says the answer doesn't matter and I'm just to stop."

"She's practical that way," Rebecca said.

She left Father to it, but was still late seating herself and had to sit on the farthest end of the bench, close to Sister Yardley who would fill the chapel with her slightly sharp and unpleasant tremolo when it came time to sing. Rebecca was impressed that she never got away with a single thing, even being only a minute late—the Lord saw fit to address her every transgression immediately and often with a sense of humor. He loved her that way, she supposed, though, in her opinion, it put some limits on her moral agency.

Rebecca didn't always like having such a big church family. Some were hard to love: Sister Isaacs who cried when she said her testimony and then blew her nose with a honking sound; Brother Minder who said "ain't" and used double negatives; Sister Shepherd who got a miracle every week, it seemed, probably hogging them all for herself. But Mother loved each one of them ferociously. She talked to Rebecca about how lonely Sister Isaacs was since she'd left her family far away, and how Brother Minder told her once that he was ashamed because he had never learned to read, and how always in true need of miracles was Sister Shepherd. Mother talked about the safety such a family brought.

One good thing, Rebecca realized that morning, was that, no matter what, they must love her because God said they had to. And they did. She hadn't thought of that before, and she considered it a progression in her character that she thought of it now.

Brother Card made congregational announcements and then there was a hymn. The pipe organ, which had been hauled by oxen on a wagon nine hundred miles from Salt Lake City, was designed to make a girl sad, Rebecca decided. It moaned, it cried—one note leaned on another, as if it couldn't stand on its own. Sister Williams played that organ like she wanted to make the prairie itself sorry to be. Had she forgotten the world was meant to be beautiful?

Throughout the hymn, the benediction, the sacrament, Rebecca sat still, watching her brothers. Gideon's thoughts most likely got no farther than the pew in front of him, where Philemon sat. He worshipped nothing more today, Rebecca guessed, than Philemon's bonnet and the curls escaping it. Zach was looking at the back of Florence Andreeson's head, disapprovingly Rebecca suspected, because of her outspoken ways. Ammon stared straight ahead and when Rebecca glanced at LaRue, she saw her sneaking glances at him. If Ammon noticed, it was beyond Rebecca's ability to detect. Radonna, she saw, watched Levi in the same way.

When church was over, the women drifted out, lighthearted from their worship. Rebecca was only light in the stomach from hunger.

She found Father talking to Brother Sempel in the churchyard.

"I must ask you again to mend your fences and keep your stock on your own land," Father was saying.

Brother Sempel grinned. "I've told and told those cows not to wander, but they don't speak English."

"I want to be neighborly," Father said, "but it's as good as stealing to let your stock graze another man's land."

"Well, then, call in the Mounties," Brother Sempel said. "Maybe the cows would understand *their* English."

He chuckled. Father did not.

"I will not involve the Mounties in the matter," Father said. "Surely we should be united before those outside the faith, who are looking for reasons to rid themselves of us. But it is my intention to find a resolution to this."

"Pray about it, Brother Leavitt," Sempel said with a wry smile, "and perhaps God will provide a way." And he stomped off.

Rebecca walked to the wagon and wondered what the reason was for church. There was Father who smoked and there were her people who could be hard to love, and there was herself just as she was when a Visit should have made her better. There was Brother Sempel, who wasn't much like a brother, or perhaps too much like a brother, but to be fair there was also Levi with his manly "amens" and Coby, his face full of the words of the speaker.

And then there he was, walking beside her.

"Coby," she said.

"I'm taking on extra work, driving freight to where they're building the railroad from Lethbridge south to Great Falls—food and other supplies. There's good money in it. Ammon will keep an eye out for my stock, but I wonder if I could ask you to feed my chickens and milk my cow. You may have the milk and butter of it, of course."

She knew she should do it for free—but there was the

matter of four hundred eighty dollars to be earned. She could earn money selling that milk and butter.

"Deal," she said, holding out her hand.

He shook her hand and smiled, and kept shaking it. He looked at his hand still shaking hers as if he couldn't believe it was misbehaving in this way. He pulled it away, and turned and left.

She watched after him, wondering why he was doing all this extra work when he had his homestead to care for, but she supposed it was none of her business.

While she was trying hard to mind her own business, Levi also stopped by her wagon and tipped his hat to her.

"How are your horses, Levi?" she said, remembering that she'd never asked him this at the dance.

"Business is going well," he said. "I have some buyers from Calgary coming this week. I was telling your father that he should think about getting you a better horse—I'd give you a good deal."

"Get rid of Tiny? I couldn't. I've had him since he was a colt."

"He's skittish, willful."

"It's true he bucks sometimes, but he always drops me in a soft spot."

"He's tetchy."

"I've figured out his ways. He blows out his belly when I'm cinching the saddle, so I just wait till he can't hold his breath anymore."

He laughed. "Good thinking. Well, if you want to come by my place sometime and have a look at my animals, you're welcome anytime," he said.

"Maybe I will. I've been told you can break any horse God made," she said.

She imagined he broke a horse the way he had taught her to waltz—with a strong hand and a commanding confidence. She couldn't help thinking of what Coby had said about his Blackfoot ponies. "I'm not much for breaking a horse's spirit," he had said. "I gentle them. There's a way to persuade a horse with love unfeigned."

That was the difference between a Coby and a Levi, she thought... She couldn't really name exactly what that difference was, only that there was one.

Then Radonna was there on her horse.

"Hello, Radonna," Levi said, tipping his hat. "Now see, Rebecca, that's a good horse."

Radonna sat a horse beautifully, Rebecca had to admit.

"Levi was just inviting me to see his horses," Rebecca said.

"I've heard admirable things about your operation," Radonna said. She turned her horse away from Rebecca, forcing Levi to follow in order to hear. "I would love to get your advice on..."

Rebecca couldn't hear how she continued.

On the way home, they passed Brother Sempel's cows feeding sweetly on their grass.

"We have been patient with this, Father," Ammon said, "or at least you have constrained us to patience. But patience has its limits. I prophesy that soon one of those beeves is going to meet an unfortunate end by gracing our Sunday dinner table."

"Easy, son," Father said. "We have to stay strong as a community and that will only happen as we exercise wisdom and judgment. You all will be guided by me in this thing."

That evening Rebecca went out to milk their cow. All was as usual in the barn. The Cat Named Dog slept in the corner. Dog was a good mouser, and delivered a dead mouse daily to Mother, fulfilling the measure of her creation. The chickens wandered in and out. And two milch cows.

Their own caramel-colored cow.

And a strange cow.

A spotty cow.

Brother Sempel's milch cow.

It was munching on what was left of their hay. Her brothers' good hay, their own sweet timothy, which they had worked so hard to grow and gather last year, the hay she had tramped down on the hayrack until her legs gave out.

"Range grass is one thing; hay is another," she said to the spotty cow.

The cow paid her not the slightest mind.

"You, cow! Go away!" Her cow swung its heavy head toward her, but Brother Sempel had spoken true—his cow did not understand English.

Rebecca looked at those bulging, veiny udders. She thought about how much butter would be in those udders and how much she could sell it for.

"There's our grass and now our hay in that milk of yours," Rebecca said aloud.

Thoughtfully she milked her family's cow, and when she was done, and her hands were cramped, she stood and gazed at the Sempel cow. Her hands may have been tired, but they were strong. Much stronger than her divine nature at that moment. She clasped her hands behind her, as if a sin or a miracle was before her and either way it was not to be touched. Would it be wrong to take just a little of that milk Sempel's cow was making out of their hay? Hadn't she helped with the haying? Didn't she need an impossible amount of money? And wouldn't extra butter to trade at the store be a start on her savings?

Of course, there was the admonition to love your neighbor. She was fairly certain Brother Sempel would struggle to see it as a loving thing, to milk his cow. On the other hand—

She stared at those Sempel udders as if they were things of great moral consequence, as if what she was about to do would be recorded by the angels, for good or ill.

She thought of her land and decided it was for good enough.

She milked Brother Sempel's cow.

Not all of it, so he wouldn't suspect.

When she was done she lured it out of the barn with a handful of alfalfa until it could see other cows. Cows were always happiest with other cows, and maybe from there it would find its way home.

Rebecca brought two buckets to the house and emptied them into the milk pans so the cream might rise.

"Mother," she called, "if I can squeeze an extra bit of butter out of the milking, might I have the profit over and above when we go to sell it in town?"

Mother said, "It will make a good beginning."

DOMINION DAY

Rebecca milked Coby's cow and collected eggs, but the coins she made from them rattled around mournfully in the black box and only made it seem emptier. So whenever she was not helping Mother, she also made straw bonnets to sell at the Dominion Day celebration. Brother Card wanted anyone and everyone to know that his people were good loyal Canadians, so of course they would celebrate Dominion Day on July 1 in Cardston in fine style. He also extended friendly invitations to less-friendly people in other communities to join the festivities, if they should wish to come.

To make the bonnets, Rebecca soaked wheat straw in alum water to bleach and soften the straw, then sliced each hollow straw into five pieces with Father's smallest, sharpest knife. Each piece must be carefully braided, then sewn together and pressed. Finally, she trimmed the crown with ribbon, and the brim with tiny pink and blue and white fabric flowers. The whole time she was making them, she thought how once she had her land and the Sitting Rock all to herself, she would never wear a bonnet at all.

The morning of Dominion Day, Rebecca was up with Mother to prepare the family picnic, and especially to prepare the food for the box lunch social Rebecca would attend for the first time with the other young people. She picked celery and small sweet onions and new potatoes from the garden for the potato salad, and made fresh mayonnaise for it. Once Mother said the oven was the right temperature—Rebecca could never tell—she baked a chocolate cake in it. Mother had opened her precious box of chocolate brick for the occasion. Then Rebecca cut up a chicken, breaded it, and fried it in lots of fresh butter after Mother got the cookstove to just the right temperature. Generally Rebecca wasn't good at cooking, except for making bread dough, and Mother said it was because she wasn't used to the cookstove. Each one had its own peculiarities, she said, and it was just a matter of getting used to them.

Once the food was in the icebox, Rebecca decorated her box. She was determined to make her box as pretty as she knew how.

"Might I use the cream-colored crepe in which you fold your wedding gloves, Mother?" Rebecca asked. "I can ask whoever unwraps it to be careful so I can bring it back to you."

"If you will be careful, yes," Mother said.

"And I think I might use one of my pale green silk hair ribbons for the bow, and I have found some wild lilies growing nearby. I shall have to pick them minutes before we leave—"

"That would be a lovely idea," Mother said.

"I wonder who will get mine?" Rebecca said.

"The luckiest one," Mother replied.

Father and her brothers finished their chores and washed up and got the horses up to the wagon. Rebecca wore a new dress Mother had sewn for the very day—a sensible gray cotton dress, but it fit her perfectly. Rebecca also wore a bonnet of her own making, one without Tarleton flowers but with a blue ribbon band that Mother said exactly matched her eyes.

"It's too bad Coby won't be back from hauling freight in time for the box lunch social." Rebecca said, "but he said he may make it later in the day." She would have liked to have shown him her pretty box. But it was Levi she hoped to eat with.

Before going to the mown field where the festivities would take place, Rebecca asked to be dropped off at the Cardston Mercantile so she could sell her butter and eggs. It was money in her pocket, but it was so very much not adding up to four hundred eighty dollars. Or even forty-eight.

Once she was done she found Father and Gideon settling the horses and Mother talking to Brother Sempel, asking where she could find his wife. He said she had elected to stay home. Rebecca asked why anybody would stay home on Dominion Day, but Brother Sempel was already walking away. Mother looked grim but told Rebecca, "You go have a nice time. I'll sell your bonnets."

The field where the Dominion Day festivities would take place was next to the baseball diamond. It was already surrounded by horses and wagons—drays with their neatly tucked-in wheels, a few pony runabouts, and a dashing trap. People had arrived from Frankburg, Pot Hole, and Fish Creek. A small stage had been erected, as well as makeshift tents, open to the stage, for babies and the elderly to rest in.

There would be rodeo events: bucking broncos and bull-riding and calf-roping, and sheep-riding for the little boys. There would be speeches and recitations. There would be a variety show, and competitions for best layer cake and plumpest calves and finest horseflesh. There would be races, both foot and saddle, and the Jensens would make ice cream with ice saved in sawdust all winter and spring long. And there were things to buy: lace collars, aprons, small wooden toys... and bonnets.

Rebecca took her decorated box, wrapped in a tea towel so nobody would see what it looked like, to the small shelter that had been made by draping quilts over a table and was cooled with precious blocks of ice. Just as she took the towel off to tuck the box into the shelter, Radonna and Levi appeared at her side.

"We mustn't look," Radonna said, covering her eyes dramatically, though Rebecca was sure they had seen her box.

"Radonna, Levi," Rebecca said, nodding.

"Yes, we've come together," Radonna said meaningfully, placing her hand briefly on Levi's arm.

Levi touched the brim of his hat. "Would you like to walk with us, Rebecca?"

She would, but before she could say so, Radonna said, "No, she must go away while I take the towel off my box lunch, and you must look away, too, Levi."

Levi looked away and Rebecca went away.

The festivities began with everyone singing "God Save the Queen," and Brother Card making a speech.

Then came the baseball game between the church team and the Cochrane cowboys' team. Levi and Rebecca's brothers were on the church team, and the consensus was they won. Nobody could be too sure, however, because the game ended in a fight, as they often did. A baseball game wasn't a baseball game, Ammon said, without a good ol' fight.

After things calmed down the Dominion Day celebration began in earnest.

Rebecca saw that a group of people were huddled around Joe Cosley, who was weeping and explaining that his Montana sweetheart didn't want to marry him. Though he was clearly in mourning, he still wore his bright hat with the embroidered flowers on the underside of the brim.

"So what are you going to do with the ring?" someone asked.

"Well, gents," he replied, "I have hung it from the branch of a tree in the mountains, along one of the trails."

A brief silence, and then a collective intake of breath.

"Isn't that ring worth two thousand dollars?"

"It is, and it's free for the taking if anyone can find it," Joe said. "I've carved my initials in the very tree, but then I've carved my initials into a hundred trees along those trails."

Two thousand dollars! She could buy her land outright four times over with that much money!

Rebecca looked among the crowd for LaRue to tell her about the ring, and finally found her with several of her little brothers in tow. The oldest, Ormus, was holding a tray of candy apples.

"A penny each," he said, holding the tray before Rebecca. "They're last year's apples but they taste good with Mother's caramel on them. One of them is special. Pick one if you dare."

"I always take a dare," Rebecca said. One of the apples was larger than the others, but she chose the smallest. "The smallest are always the sweetest," she said. She gave Ormus a penny.

"Oh, too bad, Rebecca," Ormus said. "You didn't get the special one. It's an onion, you know." He seemed to think Rebecca should feel unlucky about this.

"Well, I'm disappointed," she said, ruffling his hair.

"Now, boys," LaRue said, "you might go play with the other children, so long as you stay away from the horses."

"We will, LaRue," they said, and ran off, except Ormus. Her brothers obeyed LaRue because they couldn't stand her disapproval. If any one of them disobeyed and got himself killed doing some fool thing, the rest would have to kill him again for breaking their sister's heart.

"So, did you put your box lunch under the table, LaRue?"

"I did," she said. A small pink blotch formed on her neck. "Did Ammon bring a little money?"

"There's the danger he will love you and marry you, you know."

"If only such danger were possible."

"Be grateful. The Lord is saving you."

"Oh, Rebecca, why are you so hard on him?"

Before Rebecca could answer, Radonna and Levi and a few others joined them.

"Hello, LaRue," Radonna said sweetly. "And there you are again, Rebecca," she said less sweetly. "Oh, I do love a candy apple," she said to Ormus.

"A penny each," he said.

Radonna looked expectantly at Levi, who produced a penny. Something about that penny infuriated Rebecca.

Radonna reached out and chose the biggest, roundest, most perfect caramel apple of all. She bit down through the caramel and—

With a squeal she spit it out.

"What the hell—!" She slapped her hand over her mouth and looked at Levi looking at her, and Rebecca couldn't tell which one was more surprised.

"It's an onion, Levi!" Radonna cried.

Rebecca knew she would always have that moment in her memory, preserved like bright berries in a glass jar, Radonna spitting and cursing, and realizing that she had just spit and cursed in front of Levi. She thought for a moment that she heard angels singing, though it might have been some women taken to the stage to entertain the company.

"I was going to say, there was a special one," Ormus said, confused about why no one was laughing. Standing behind him, LaRue put her hands protectively on his shoulders.

One did not laugh in the face of a miracle, but Rebecca couldn't help it. She put her hand over her mouth to stop herself, but it could not be contained. Ormus seemed relieved that somebody got it.

"You're a naughty child," Radonna said to Ormus.

Ormus looked stricken, and LaRue pulled him closer to her.

Levi managed to smile and look regretful at the same time. "Well now, Radonna, you did choose that one, and I'm sure no permanent damage was done."

Rebecca should have repented of her gloating right then, but how could she, in the face of a blessing of unhoped-for proportions?

Radonna glared at Rebecca as if she herself had served up the onion apple, then stumped away in a most unlady-like fashion. Levi followed at a small distance, and Rebecca thought it really must be the singing of angels she could hear.

Ormus went off to sell the rest of his unsurprising cara-mel apples, and Rebecca and LaRue made their way to a quieter part of the grounds where the box lunch social was being staged. The social was one of the highlights of Dominion Day, so although participation was restricted to those of marriageable age, some younger and older came to watch. The bidding money would go to expanding the church building, which discouraged, it seemed, the partici-pation of anyone not of their faith.

By the rules of the box lunch social, the bidder was not to know whose lunch he had purchased until after the last lunch had been sold. One by one, then, the blushing girls would find their box and the young man who possessed it, and the girl and the bidder would eat its contents together. Rebecca hoped beyond hope that somehow Levi would bid on her box.

The girls all stood together in a troop to one side, with Minnie and Lyla and LaRue in between Rebecca and Radonna. It was well known that Minnie was already an accomplished cook, so lucky the one who bid on her box. Lyla was so sweet-tempered that anyone would find the food in her box delicious just because of her company.

When Brother Card, as auctioneer, held up the first box for all to admire, Rebecca overheard Radonna confess that it was hers. Radonna must have found a way to let Levi know which box was hers, for he immediately began to bid for it.

"One dollar," Levi called.

"I have one dollar," Brother Card called. "Do I hear one and two bits?"

"A whole dollar," Jolene said, giggling. "How he must love you, Radonna."

"One fifty," called Henry Dickenson.

"Henry is bidding!" Jolene said to Radonna in surprise. "Why, isn't he your second cousin? Won't he be disappointed to find he has purchased the lunch of a relation!"

Radonna smiled. "He owes me a favor. I told him he could repay me were he to bid Levi up a little. We don't want Levi to think I come too cheaply, now, do we?"

In the end, Levi got Radonna's box for a dollar and seventy-five cents, a generous sum for a box lunch, and which he could have, Rebecca said to LaRue, spent on a good pair of boots. Much of the shine went out of the social, then, for Rebecca, but there was still the mystery of who would get her box.

When LaRue's box came up, Rebecca knew it was hers

because her neck began to burst into bloom, though her face stayed still and inscrutable.

"Now here's a pretty box, gents!"

It was wrapped in a square of light blue gingham. The ribbon was simple twine, but trapped in the twine were fresh white daisies with pale yellow hearts, and one wild rose: without pretense, modest, but somehow the best of all. Just like LaRue. Rebecca thought that if the men knew it was LaRue's, they'd be bidding fast and high.

Ammon said calmly but for all to hear, "Ninety-five cents. That's all I got, except for a punch in the nose for whoever bids higher."

LaRue's neck suddenly went white as a pillar.

"He knows it's yours," Rebecca whispered.

"But how? I didn't cheat."

"No," Rebecca said, "you never would." She didn't, however, put it past Ammon.

"Now, now, punching is against the rules, young Brother Leavitt," Brother Card said to Ammon. "Any other bidders, gentlemen?"

But no one seemed to want the box for a dollar and a punch in the nose, so Ammon claimed the box. LaRue grasped Rebecca's hand.

It raised her brother in Rebecca's esteem to think that he had the good taste to know that if any girl were worth cheating for, it was LaRue.

One by one all the people Rebecca might have enjoyed eating lunch with had boxes in hand, so her expectations were low. Radonna glowed, and Rebecca assumed it must be because her box had gone for the highest bid of the day to Levi, the most gallant of the gentlemen. But there was something else in her expression, Rebecca thought— something watchful or expectant. And when Brother Card took her box out from under the shelter, she knew why.

Rebecca's beautiful box was beautiful no longer.

"Now I've been saving this box till last because it's clear it met up with an accident of some kind." He raised it to the view of all.

It was still covered in the creamy crepe she had taken from Mother's glove box, but the fabric had been smudged with dirt. The flowers had been plucked from their stems, the green ribbon hung frayed and bedraggled. The box was crumpled and looked like it had been kicked across the prairie to the social.

Radonna was the only one who would have known which box was hers—and Levi. No one else had seen. She turned toward Radonna, who looked at her with a small smile. Yes, Radonna had ruined it. And it was only fair, given Rebecca's glee at her display earlier. Deed for deed, the consequences of sin, as Mother would say. Still, Rebecca was alarmed to feel something like she might want to cry. That was against the rules, to cry—that was so against the Leavitt rules. One took one's licks, and that was that.

"I wonder whose it is?" LaRue said sadly.

"It's mine," Rebecca said.

Loman called out, "Brother Card, what will you pay me to bid on that box?"

Laughter.

"Now, now, gentlemen," Brother Card said, "let us not

judge the food within by the packaging without. What will you bid for this lunch?"

"I got a plug-ugly nickel here I might part with!" Royal called out.

More laughter.

Rebecca stood tall. She would not flinch before her just deserts. The more they laughed, the taller she stood.

"Now, gents, somewhere in this party is a young lady who belongs to this box, and we don't want to injure her feelings with too much hilarity. Who will bid a quarter for this box, for which there is surely some explanation? Fifteen cents? Ten?"

"Ten cents," called LeVar, who was known for his thrifty ways among a people known for their thrift, and had probably been waiting all afternoon for such a bargain.

"Ten cents!" Brother Card called, pointing to LeVar. "Who will give me fifteen?"

Rebecca did not avert her gaze.

"Ten cents once, twice—"

"Three dollars!"

The crowd made a collective sound of astonishment, and Radonna's voice rose above them all. You could buy a hundred-pound bag of flour for three dollars!

"Who said that?" Brother Card asked, craning his neck.

"I did."

Levi stepped forward out of the crowd. "Don't know any rule that says I can't buy two lunches if I want."

Brother Card smiled. "Nor do I. And did I hear right, Levi, that you bid three dollars for this box?"

"I did."

"Sold! The highest bid of the day goes to the last bid of the day. Ladies, please find your boxes and enjoy lunch with your gentlemen."

Rebecca had been standing so stiffly, she could hardly unbend herself to walk toward Levi, who now held the bedraggled box. "It was mine," she said. What she wanted to say was, Thank you. She wanted to say, You are the kindest man. She wanted to say she was going to be good for the rest of her life, now.

"I recognized it from its former glory, I admit," he said to her. "It was a mean job of it, whoever did it."

Radonna joined them, carrying a quilt over her arm.

"Oh, it was your box, Rebecca, poor thing! Wasn't Levi the gentleman to rescue you. You must join us. Here, share our quilt." She had an ice cream voice, at once sweet and cold.

"Thank you," Rebecca said, kneeling on the quilt.

"I'm sure the inside is good," Levi said to Rebecca, placing her bedraggled box on the quilt.

Rebecca said quietly, "Fried chicken and potato salad and chocolate cake..."

Radonna spoke over her as she unpacked her box lunch, telling Levi she had made the quilt herself, and how many compliments she'd had at the bee because she'd done ten stitches to the inch. She settled her skirts around her and placed her box before Levi.

"I have enough for the three of us, Rebecca. You have so many hungry mouths at home that you'll surely be welcomed home with lunch intact."

Radonna was chatty and kept Levi's full attention while she handed out beef sandwiches on great slabs of home-made bread and butter, fresh new radishes, and the most beautiful mock apple pie Rebecca had ever seen. Levi deserved such a mock pie.

"And there are no onions in it, not even a little bit," Radonna said cheerily, as if to say they could all laugh about it now.

Rebecca couldn't find any way to join the conversation, which was about who might be beaux, and how so-and-so might be feeling about eating lunch with such-and-such when he had really been hoping for the box of thee-and-thou. Rebecca noticed that Gideon and Philemon had not bothered with the auction, but Philemon had brought an enormous picnic basket for him anyway. LaRue and Ammon were talking as if they were the only ones in the world. Royal had got Florence Andreeson's box, and since she was three inches taller than him, and three times smarter than him, Rebecca guessed he wasn't enjoying his lunch as much as he had hoped. Zach had got the lunch of sweet and simpering Libby, which seemed lucky for him, but Zach was talking mostly with Florence on the blanket next to his, leaving Libby talking mostly with Royal. She wondered what Zach would have to say to Florence—probably scolding her for her opinions on suffrage. That was the thing about box lunch socials, Rebecca thought—you stood to be miserable or joyous and not much in between.

As Radonna and Levi chatted, Rebecca stared at the mountains and consoled herself by thinking about how she would always be known as the girl whose box lunch had sold for three dollars, purchased by none other than Levi Howard.

"You're awfully quiet, Rebecca," he said.

"Levi," Rebecca said, "have you ever had a miracle?"

"You mean like making the blind to see?"

"Yes, like that. Or . . . seeing angels . . . or suchlike."

"Never seen a miracle. Never seen the dead get raised, only lowered. Never met a blind man who got to see again."

"Well," said Radonna as she began packing up, "I hear that Rebecca's mother gets knocking angels." She said it with a forkish smile.

"Does she now," Levi said. "Never saw an angel, either, knocking or otherwise."

Nothing could spoil Rebecca's peace.

"The mountains are like miracles," she said.

"What, those old things?" Levi said, but she was sure he looked at them with the same love she did.

"The queen never imagined such mountains as ours," Rebecca said.

"She's not my queen," Levi said. "A man in this part of the world is king of himself."

"Or this grass," Rebecca said. "This grass is almost a miracle, you know." She gestured to the prairie that stretched away to the south.

"Grass?" Radonna said.

"Father taught me that this here is buffalo grass—fescue as they call it. Used to grow wild over this whole country before the white man came along. The leaves of the fescue, they're shaped so's the water, when it rains, or when it dews, it gets funneled on down right into the heart of the plant. All the dead stuff of the previous years, it soaks up that water and holds on to it for drought times. And the roots, they go down four feet deep, so when the wildfires come, it can grow back without a blink. But cows eat it down instead of moving on like the buffalo did, so the roots grow shallow and die, and we have to grow hay. I'd like to let that grass be, just keep it wild, a place for the critters to come."

"It would be a shame," Levi said, "to let such land go to waste. It could be counted a miracle what a man can do with such a wilderness as this."

Radonna, appearing bored by the conversation, stood.

"Well, I'm sure I'd love to talk more about grass, Levi, but we should hurry to the corral," she said. "We don't want to miss the horse judging, especially since you'll likely be the winner. I'll need my blanket, Rebecca." She tugged at it before Rebecca was quite on her feet and she had to catch her balance ungracefully.

Rebecca plunked herself down again on the grass and watched them walk away with just the tiniest seed of resentment, which quickly grew to uncharitable feelings of the keenest kind. Rebecca told herself that she should not indulge in thoughts of Radonna stepping into a steaming cow pie or getting a click beetle in her hair or tripping in a foot race or dripping mustard or ice cream or both on her pink silk dress...

She sighed.

Brother Card walked by.

"Eating alone, Rebecca?"

"Brother Card, why do girls cook and boys bid? I say next year we do it backwards."

"Why Rebecca," he said with a pleasant smile, "boys don't cook."

"Then let them make medicine and have a taste of their own, sir," she said.

Rebecca turned away from the Dominion Day festivities and faced the south prairie, and, beyond that, Chief Mountain. The flat-topped mountain was black against the hot blue sky. It was called "Ninastako" or "Chief Mountain" by the Blackfoot Confederacy, and they considered it sacred. Suddenly Coby sat beside her on the grass.

"Made it," he said.

"You did. Have you made a lot of money moving that freight?"

"Enough so I can pay Ammon for watching my stock and still make a profit."

"I wish you could have made it to the box lunch social. You would have seen Levi save me," Rebecca said.

"It was gallant of him," Coby said when she had explained.

"Did you eat already?" she asked.

"No."

"Here then. Radonna made Levi eat her lunch so he didn't eat any of mine."

"Thank you," he said, and he lit in, saying with his mouth full how delicious it was.

While he ate, Rebecca thought again how Levi had bid three whole dollars for her box lunch. Levi, a waltzer, a tipper of hats, and able to put up his dukes in a fight, had been a hero to her.

Showy clouds were blowing over the mountain peaks, and pretty ponds that weren't really there shimmered on the prairie. The wind ran like wild horses in the grass.

Levi, she thought, was a beautiful thing, a fine horse, a lumber house, as compared to, say, a man like Coby. Coby was a barn. Coby was practical, warm, and safe, but having to be mucked out every so often. The barn might lean or fade, but you never fussed about it. You couldn't do without a barn, but it wasn't a temple, or a Greek statue. That was Levi—something high, something special, that you went to by invitation, something you could do without but you wouldn't want to. Something...romantic.

The conversation on the way home that night was all about the success of the Dominion Day celebration, which one of the Mounties said was the best in the territory. After the shortest family prayer ever, they went to bed. Mother came into Rebecca's bedroom with her candle and silently put some money on the windowsill. "Your bonnets," she said. "Between this and the butter in town, you've got a bit of a sum."

Rebecca got out her black enameled money box and added the bonnet money.

"Thank you, Mother."

She stared into the box. She wouldn't count it—not yet. But it was more money than she'd ever had. Still, butter and eggs and bonnets would never earn her the amount she needed.

Mother sat on the side of her bed. "I heard what happened with your box lunch."

"It was nothing more than I deserved. I'm afraid the crepe is ruined."

Mother shook her head. "Never mind that."

Rebecca wanted to ask her mother about Greek statues, but Mother kissed her forehead and left the room, shutting the door ever so silently.

Rebecca put her money box on the shelf. It would take a miracle for her to be a ten-stitch-per-inch girl, or to be as good as LaRue and Mother, and perhaps those were the miracles she should be praying for. But the miracle she really wanted was her land.

MIDWIFERY

Whenever Rebecca went to Coby's to feed the chickens and milk the cows, she went by way of the tor and took a little time to sit on the Sitting Rock and gaze at the mountains and pretend it was her Sitting Rock. It reminded her, being there, that wonderful things could happen. Sometimes she planned what she would say were the Wonderful Thing ever to happen again.

There was no scrimping on the work at home. Monday was laundry, Tuesday ironing, Wednesday baking, Thursday cleaning, Friday sewing and mending, and Saturday baking again: this in addition to always cooking and cleaning up after meals, milking, making beds, sweeping, slopping pigs, robbing the chickens, and hauling water. Sundays no work was done, except for caring for the animals. Cows didn't observe the Sabbath.

In summer there was the additional work of gardening and bottling, and all the hoarding that must be done before winter came. Sometimes there was also soapmaking and candle-making.

Rebecca had stopped complaining years ago because of the eleventh commandment, but now she tried not to complain in her heart. She tried to be willing to help Mother, but often found herself dreaming about wandering on Tiny, or fishing and hiking in the mountains — and knew she was just pretending to be willing in those times. She hoped that pretending counted for something.

Early one summer morning, not long after Dominion Day, Mother stopped her work, looked toward the door, and started preparing a cold supper for her family.

Rebecca knew what that meant. Father and her brothers knew, too, and looked a bit glum.

Mother always knew ahead of time when she would be called upon to go to a birth because she would be warned by one bold, sharp rap at the door. When it first started to happen, years before, when Mother was young, she would check to see if anyone was at the door. No one was there. Time after time, no one was there. But sure as sure, in another hour or two or three, another knock would come, from the husband or an older child, hesitant, a little desperate.

"My wife is sick," the husband would say.

Mother used the words *in labor* and *pregnant* because she was a midwife, but other people refrained from such language.

My wife is sick, and "I am ready," Mother would say. She always was.

Mother had come to realize that the knock she heard, but which nobody else in the family ever heard, was the knock of an angel, come to tell her to get ready to be away from her family.

"How do you know? Have you seen an angel on our porch?" Rebecca had asked.

"No," Mother said. "But I know one is there. If I open the door out of doubt, it shows I'm not firm-minded enough to see an angel."

"But if you don't open the door, you won't see the angel, either."

"It's a puzzle," Mother said cheerfully.

That knock, that one bold, sharp rap, Mother said, was how she knew angels were not timid things—there was no apology in that knock. Up. Up and ready, it said.

So Rebecca knew, when Mother stopped her work that day and made a cold supper for the men, what had happened. Mother gathered her small bag of midwifing instruments.

"And now I have a few minutes to discipline my mind to gratitude for the opportunity to serve," Mother said.

It was good of her to be grateful, Rebecca thought, for not all could afford to recompense her for her time and skill. But, it suddenly occurred to Rebecca, some could and did.

"I am coming to help you," Rebecca said. Now she had said it. She hadn't meant it, but she had said it, and she would do it.

Mother looked at her in astonishment, and just then the other knock came.

It was Brother Ashford, hat in hands. "My wife," said he.

"You are to witness a sacred thing, daughter," Mother said as they rode their horses up to the Ashford cabin.

The Ashford home was a humble place, though it boasted a Magee Grand cookstove that cost dear. Sister

Ashford had cleverly made a dresser out of coal-oil cases and curtained it with handmade lace, in order that the rest of the kitchen might live up to the stove. On a shelf, she displayed a pretty platter among the tins and sacks and everyday things. The platter showed a river with a little boat and a wooden bridge, willows on the bank, and a castle in the distance. This was surely England, Rebecca thought, but she found it all rather doll-like compared to the grandeur of the Territories.

Sister Ashford was in bed, and her husband stood about mutely like a sick horse, somehow always in the way, until Mother said it would be a long time and didn't he have work to do and wouldn't he like to take his boy with him to do the chores. He said he surely did and would, and fled the house with his young son in tow.

Mother talked quietly with Sister Ashford about her pains, showing great sympathy.

"When God took a rib out of Adam, he put him to sleep," Mother said, "allowing no such accommodation for women." To Rebecca she said, "I have heard of the new knowledge called bacteriology. They say now that childbed fever is caused by the contamination of unwashed hands to the mother. But of course God knew this all along, for we wash, and we anoint the laboring mother, and we do not lose them."

Rebecca watched as her mother performed the rites of washing and anointing, and listened to the words of the blessing as she placed her hands on Sister Ashford's head. The blessing promised strength and endurance to the mother and the good health of the baby.

When the laboring woman's pains became stronger, and Mother saw Rebecca's distress about it, she said, "You might look around and see what can be done about the house."

"I have. The house is spick-and-span."

"Just do what needs you most," she answered, and Rebecca found a small basket of ironing to do.

Rebecca thought, after an hour or so, that the woman had been punished enough for what made the baby in the first place. But then it went on. And on. Mother said encouraging things, and Sister Ashford moaned, and Rebecca decided that any man who protested love for a woman was a liar next to the woman who bore his child, unless he stood to die for it.

Several hours later Sister Ashford said she thought she was seeing beyond the veil. Mother said calmly, "I am here to bring you back." Mother put a cool damp cloth on her forehead.

After what seemed endless suffering, after airing her bare bottom, after sweating and moaning, after every conceivable indignity, Rebecca thought, the baby at last was born.

Mother cut the cord and the afterbirth was expelled and even then the indignities were not over, for the baby must nurse at the breast, and Rebecca was astonished at how very cow-like it all was.

"So what do you think, Rebecca?" Mother said quietly when Sister Ashford was cooing over her baby.

"I think I shall never have a baby," she replied.

She was just about to ask Mother if she might go home

and clean the house and mend the socks and clean out the stove and fill the woodbox and polish the kerosene lamps and do any number of chores so she might be away, when Brother Ashford came to the door.

"Come in, Brother Ashford, and meet your new son," Mother said. "And Will, you must meet your brother."

Sister Ashford smiled weakly at her husband, which Rebecca thought the greatest act of Christian forgiveness she had witnessed.

"He's as fat as a piglet," Brother Ashford said with wonder.

Rebecca didn't believe that men really loved their babies, but she thought Brother Ashford was making a convincing show of it.

The baby's brother, Will, was frowning at the scene of family love before him, standing apart from everyone, refusing to be drawn in.

"Come, Will," his mother said. "Come see your brother."

He shook his head and crossed his arms over his chest.

Rebecca knew a kindred spirit when she saw one. She knelt by him.

"What do you think?" Rebeca asked.

He pointed at the baby. "I don't want that."

"Are you sure?"

"I'm sure enough."

"Shall I throw it in the ash heap, then?"

The boy looked at Rebecca as if she were the only sensible person in the world, and surely the only one who understood him. He nodded.

Rebecca went to the mother and took the baby from her

arms as casually as she might a cat. Sister Ashford gasped a little, but Mother held a hand up, as if to say, wait and see.

Rebecca opened the door and the wind came on in.

She heaved the baby back, as if she were getting ready for a good ol' toss.

"Wait!" Will called.

"Yes?"

"Maybe not."

"Are you sure?"

"Maybe tomorrow," he said.

"Well, I'd best hand it over before I get tempted."

Sister Ashford took the baby back with a possessive joy. Rebecca had thought a mother a soft thing, but now she knew this was not true. This mother had suffered bravely and was as fiercely protective as any wild-animal mother: wary and ready, tooth-and-claw ready.

Will stayed by his mother's side to examine the baby at his leisure.

Rebecca decided that if she could find a way to avoid the expulsion of babies, she wouldn't mind having a child like Will.

When Mother released her, she went straight to LaRue's house. LaRue had seen her coming and sent her younger brothers off to the haystack with a tea towel full of fresh-made cinnamon buns.

The girls sat in the grass where they could see the creek and the mountains. The daylight sky was tinged with pink. The grass was decorated with fringed purple gentian and white shooting stars and Johnny-jump-ups. The air was soft as it never was, and the mountains swept up blue out of the prairie. An eagle flew before the face of the mountains, the smallest speck of an eagle. It was joined by its mate, and they floated like dust motes.

"You seem happy, LaRue."

She looked down and smiled. "Ammon came by earlier to show the boys a buffalo skull he'd found."

"Hmm," Rebecca said. "Came to see the boys, did he?"

LaRue continued smiling and didn't answer.

Rebecca told her about Sister Ashford's baby. "I have come to you to mourn my forever-unborn children. I know I shall never have babies."

"But I'm afraid, Rebecca," LaRue said, "that babies cannot be stopped."

"They can if one knows the mechanism of it, which I do."

LaRue rarely betrayed alarm at Rebecca's confessions, but now her neck flushed up like a summer sunset.

They were silent together in the grass, staring ahead at the creek. They could hear the boys hollering at the haystack.

LaRue put a comforting hand on Rebecca's arm. "It is God's will, Rebecca. He made us to have babies."

Rebecca covered her friend's hand gently with her own.

"We like to blame everything on him," Rebecca said, and it was the closest she had ever come to contradicting her friend.

"Well, anyway, babies are nice," LaRue said softly, which was the closest she had ever come to contradicting back.

After a brief silence, LaRue tried again. "Mother says that Mother Eve knew what she was doing when she ate the forbidden fruit."

"Well," said Rebecca, "Mother Eve made her choice, and I have made mine. I shall neither multiply nor replenish—" She stopped and thought that Levi probably had opinions about babies.

Just then LaRue's little brothers came loping toward the house, calling like gulls, the littlest at the tail end. Her mother came to the door in her Mother Hubbard dress, meaning she was going to have another baby.

"Rebecca, you're welcome to stay for supper!"

"Stay for supper, Rebecca?" LaRue said.

"Thank you, but I need to go home for chores."

The girls embraced, and Rebecca rode for home.

She was a bit low in spirits when she arrived, realizing she would never be as good as Mother, who saw midwifing as something sacred. But when she arrived, on the porch was a chicken in a box. An unfamiliar chicken.

Mother said, "It's a gift for you from Brother Ashford, for helping to deliver his new son. More eggs to sell in town."

Rebecca had never before met a chicken she liked, but she decided she liked this one very well.

Mother brought Rebecca with her to two more deliveries that month. She listened to her mother's instructions to the laboring women, her calm, steadying words, but stayed mostly in the shadows, cleaning, caring for children, milking, feeling sorry for the mother, and thinking that Mother Eve might have brokered a better deal for her daughters.

Gifts arrived not long after—another laying hen and a goose. Both Mother gave to Rebecca for her "savings," and Rebecca began to warm to the idea of midwifing as her black enameled money box acquired a little heft.

Just after breakfast one day near the beginning of August, Mother quietly stopped her work and started preparing her midwife's bag. Of course, Rebecca had heard nothing, not the smallest knock, but soon after Leila Manwell came to the door. Rebecca loved to look at Leila, who was about ten years old. She had fat, glossy, chestnut braids that went all the way to her waist, and her face and arms were covered in tiny freckles, as if God had painted them on one at a time with the brush of a single hair. She was wearing a floppy straw hat that she snatched off when Mother came to the door.

"Sister Leavitt, my mother has gone to bed."

"Hello, Leila. I am ready."

"Sister Manwell's house is full of daughters to help," Mother said to Rebecca. "You may stay home and take care of the sewing today."

Mother left, her father and brothers were gone to the fields, and Rebecca pretended she was queen of the house. She picked and arranged wildflowers in a vase and thought how she could be alone whenever she wished when she had her own land. She was lost in her imaginings when the door opened and there stood LaRue.

"LaRue!" She embraced her friend for she never could help it.

LaRue had come away without her bonnet, and her braids had escaped their ties.

"Come in, come in!" But from LaRue's expression, Rebecca quickly knew this was no ordinary visit. "Is everything all right?"

"It's Mama, Rebecca—it's her time. I've come to fetch your mother."

"But—but Mother is at Manwells' for a delivery!"

LaRue's neck turned a blue-white, like snow on the coldest of days. "What will I do?"

"We must go get Sister Ashford to come," Rebecca said, taking off her apron.

"I went by her house on the way here, asking her to stay with Mother while I went to fetch your mother. But she was afraid she would have to do something, and she said having a baby wasn't at all like midwifing one, and that even you knew more than her and I should just hurry on my way..."

"Sister Sempel?"

They looked at each other in silence. No, not Sister Sempel, who had never had a child and who, when she made an appearance at all, always looked ghostlike, frail and floaty and not quite there.

"It shall have to be you, Rebecca."

"LaRue, I don't know anything! I don't even know what I don't know!"

"I'll find someone else, but please go to her while I do. Father's taken the boys fishing in the mountains."

Rebecca searched her heart. How many times had she vowed she would walk across the plains, barefoot in winter, for her friend, if she needed her? And now, when for the first time LaRue needed her for something, would she say no?

"LaRue, I will go to your mother if you will go to mine and tell her. She'll know what to do."

"Yes!" LaRue said. "That's exactly what we should do." She put her hands on Rebecca's shoulders. "That is my Rebecca—not afraid of anything."

Mother had taken her bag, but Rebecca knew that in the dresser drawer in her mother's room were notes she had compiled on midwifing. She snatched them up, saddled Tiny, and was away.

All the way there, Rebecca confessed to her own heart that, in spite of the unspoken Leavitt creed, she was afraid of many things—summer blizzards, and stepping in a hornets nest or being eaten by a bear. And chief among her fears was childbirth, she decided, as she rode up to the Fletcher household, and not only for herself: her fear was much more democratic than that.

The upstairs of the Fletcher home had two bedrooms: a big one for all six boys, and a small one for LaRue. The downstairs was mostly kitchen, except for a small parental bedroom in the back corner. And that was where Rebecca found Sister Fletcher. The woman sat up in bed and did not welcome Rebecca with relief, as the other women had welcomed her mother.

"Where's your mother, Rebecca?"

"It's just me, ma'am. For now. But you mustn't worry—LaRue has gone to fetch Mother at Manwells'. I know she'll be here as soon as she can."

"Is it really just you, Rebecca?" Her gaze drifted past Rebecca, as if she were searching for someone who might be hiding behind her. "You, here to deliver me of a child and all my worry? Lord help me."

"He will help you, I am sure, ma'am, for you are a good woman."

"Goodness has thus far spared me little in life but a heavy conscience."

"In the meantime, Mother has made notes."

"Notes!"

A contraction must have gripped her then, for Sister Fletcher fell back onto her pillows, closed her eyes, and made a sound like something between a sigh and a moan.

Rebecca examined the notes, but they contained words and sketches that made no sense to her, as if they were in code. Where was the note that said, number one, set water to boil?

Well, Sister Fletcher had attended to that already, which was disappointing, seeing as that was the one thing Rebecca felt she could do with confidence. She continued riffling through the pages, as if they would suddenly reveal their meaning to her.

"Oh, for heaven's sake, dear, put down the notes. This is my eighth baby—I'll tell you what to do if it comes to that."

Sister Fletcher was a patient, long-suffering woman, but Rebecca detected an edge in her voice she had never heard before.

"Yes, tell me what to do," Rebecca said.

"Do nothing for now." She lay back on her pillow and closed her eyes. "When the Lord said to multiply and replenish the earth, I guess he meant for me to do it all myself. And all by myself."

Rebecca didn't do nothing. She made bread and looked out the window for signs of Mother or LaRue or even Brother Fletcher coming home with the boys. She swept and scrubbed the already-clean pine plank floors, and polished windows and picture glass, and chatted about LaRue's many perfections. Still, Sister Fletcher labored and Mother did not come. Sister Fletcher's sighs became more jagged and her moans more guttural as time wore on, and Rebecca could not find another thing to clean. She sat beside Sister Fletcher and further extolled the virtues of her daughter, while wondering all the time what was taking Mother and LaRue so long. Rebecca began to feel that it was only she and Sister Fletcher alone together in the whole world.

Suddenly Sister Fletcher cried out.

Rebecca felt in her bones the way she had when her family's house had once been struck by lightning.

"The baby's coming!" Sister Fletcher called.

"No. I'm sorry. Mother's not here."

Rebecca placed a cold cloth on Sister Fletcher's damp forehead, as if that could hold things back.

Sister Fletcher tossed the cloth away and gasped, "Something doesn't feel right, Rebecca."

Rebecca lifted the sheet. No baby head was appearing. The baby was still neatly inside.

"You must do the anointing," Sister Fletcher said, panting.

"But I've never — I never really listened..."

"Please."

"Yes. Yes, of course."

Rebecca put her hands on Sister Fletcher's head, which was damp with sweat.

"Dear Lord," Rebecca said...

She waited for the words.

"Dear Lord," she whispered, "remember the Sit we had."

And then, in a somewhat louder voice, she said, "Sister Fletcher, you mustn't die. I don't want you to die, and LaRue doesn't want you to die, and your husband must like you or you wouldn't have all these babies. And your boys — well, God doesn't want you to die, either, that's all. Why you have fallen into the hands of a light-minded excuse for a girl like myself, I hardly know. It is something with which you might negotiate at the judgment bar. But I am proposing that you delay this talk for a time in the distant future and that you stay in this mortal coil long enough to raise this baby, which will be born strong and healthy. Of course, first you must have it. As soon as Mother gets here, please. Amen."

Sister Fletcher only said, "The head!"

Somehow Rebecca knew to cup the tiny bloody head while she eased the little shoulder out. A minute later an entire baby slipped into the world.

It flung out its tiny arms, trying to grasp something, the world, perhaps, or life, or air, or love...

"It's a baby!" Rebecca said. "A real, live baby..."

The baby looked blue in places, and Rebecca saw her struggle for air as if she were drowning in it.

Rebecca rubbed the baby with a warm towel. The baby cried, cried as if the air burned going down. Sister Fletcher supervised Rebecca on how to use thread and a boiled knife to cut the umbilical cord, but Rebecca was surprised to realize she could have done it without supervision. She swaddled the baby in another towel she had warmed near the oven, and in a few more moments the baby was quiet and her eyes opened a little and she seemed to be asking, what is this? what is this?

"It's a girl," Rebecca said in wonder.

Sister Fletcher reached greedy arms for the infant.

The afterbirth came soon, and Rebecca began cleaning up.

"It's not much less mess than the pig slaughter, I know, dear," Sister Fletcher said, out of pain now, but weary.

"Never mind. This is the part I'm familiar with," Rebecca said.

"Land, I never thought I'd have another daughter," Sister Fletcher cooed. "Look at you, love . . ."

While Sister Fletcher nursed her baby, Rebecca washed up. The whole time she was thinking that she was different now. Yes, different, or maybe it was that she had forgotten some part of herself, or why she had been who she was. And all because she had seen that baby come away from her mother and breathe. She had breathed! She had pinked up so pretty! She was LaRue's little sister!

Rebecca kept leaving off her work to peer at the baby. She wanted to say, this is life, little one, this is life mortal, and it has its miseries, but it's all right, little one, because of Sunsets . . .

Mother had taught her that the price of a good woman, as described in Proverbs, was far above rubies. Rebecca didn't know the price of a ruby. She figured it was dear, perhaps not as dear as Joe Cosley's diamond engagement ring, but perhaps as much as a cow. But whatever it was, she thought, watching Sister Fletcher nurse her baby, this woman and this child were worth many rubies—and emeralds and diamonds, too.

She heard the chop of an axe and went to the door to see Coby chopping wood.

"Coby?"

"I saw your mother and LaRue coming back from Manwells'. They said to say they are on their way. I thought I'd help with the chores, if I could. Has the baby come?"

"It has! A sister for LaRue, and she's perfect. It was just me and Sister Fletcher and the baby."

"And the mother lived?" Coby said, grinning.

"It's wonderful, isn't it?"

His face softened then. His eyelashy eyes stared at her.

"It is," he said.

Something about the way he looked at her then unsettled her, as if he hadn't been looking at her forever and there was nothing to see.

Just then she saw Mother and LaRue riding up to the house. LaRue dismounted almost before the horse stopped.

"LaRue, you have a sister!" Rebecca called.

"A sister!"

She ran to her mother.

There they were, women together. Rebecca felt as if some part of her was brand-new, born right along with Abigail Rebecca Fletcher, and that old Rebecca was still inside her somewhere, wondering, who are we now?

Mother checked Sister Fletcher over and declared her to be just fine. Sister Fletcher said Mother must go back to her own family, that LaRue could do everything she could do, and anyway she would be up and at her duties the next day. Mother tried to find something to clean, but Sister Fletcher said that Rebecca had done it all and the house had never been cleaner. So they went home.

On the way, Rebecca was thinking only about what it might be to carry the child of your husband, to present to him a little person who had the same last name as him.

A few days later Brother Fletcher brought a pig.

"It's the runt," he said, "just like little Abigail."

Rebecca imagined that runty little pig, which she named Abigail, crawling right into her money box.

THE WEDDING

O ne day Gideon came come home with Philemon to announce they were getting married in September.

Philemon was such a tiny thing—Gideon could have snapped her in half by accident—but he was utterly in her thrall. He bent to the slightest exertion of her will, attended to the smallest signals that she might be weary or cold or uncomfortable. He behaved as if God had given him all his strength and muscle for no other reason than to attend to the happiness of his Philemon.

She, in turn, refused to wield her power over him and thought only about how she might help him see that he was the best man in the world. When he was close by, she drew him into every conversation, and when he was not near, half of her many sentences began with, "Gideon and I believe," or, "As I was saying to Gideon," or, "I shall have to ask Gideon..."

Gideon and Philemon were wed in a simple ceremony in the church. Philemon wore a wedding dress of blue cashmere, Rebecca guessed ten yards of it, the upper part a basque with five seams and four darts, all boned. The skirt was heavily draped over the bustle, and everywhere were puffs and folds and pleats and ball buttons.

After the proper words, Gideon and Philemon kissed.

Rebecca thought briefly what it might be like to have Levi put his lips on hers, but then she had to stop thinking about it. It made her want to lie down.

Once the ceremony was over, the pews were pushed against the walls and the reception started. Both fathers made speeches, and a wedding breakfast was laid out by both mothers.

Rebecca and LaRue talked in a corner, wondering at Philemon's beautiful dress and laughing at Gideon's bachelor friends, who stood stiff and uncomfortable. Coby held a little flowered plate and on it a little flowered piece of cake, and he looked as if it were taking all his strength to hold it before him. Levi was on his third piece of cake, and chatting easily with everyone in the church, including Radonna.

"Father says his horse ranch is doing well," Rebecca said of Levi. "And he tools beautiful leather saddles, too. Isn't he something?"

"Are you going to go talk to him?" LaRue asked.

"No. Whatever should I say to him?" Rebecca said.

LaRue was following Ammon with her eyes. By observing little signs and preferences between the two at church services and candy pulls and house parties, it had become known to all that Ammon and LaRue liked each other. The other girls stopped flirting with Ammon out of affection for LaRue, and the other boys sensed that LaRue had set her heart. When Ammon and LaRue spoke to each other in the presence of others, no one else could quite decipher what they were saying, though they never whispered. It was a low murmuring sound. Rebecca thought it might be a secret language for a world of their own making. She couldn't get over the strangeness of seeing them together. Rebecca thought she could forgive Ammon many things for having the good sense and the good taste to prefer LaRue.

Ammon came to LaRue's side, and soon they were off in conversation by themselves. Levi wandered over to Rebecca.

"You look lost in thought," he said to her.

She had been studying Father and Mother, too, who like to have outshone the newlyweds for their sweet ways toward each other. The whole room was bursting with romance.

"Father says he knew Mother would be his wife the moment he laid eyes on her, as if he'd always known it, as if it were destiny."

"I hate destiny," Levi said.

"No sense hating what is. Such as, we are all destined to die. Do you want to die when you're young, Levi, and have lots of people come to your funeral? Or when you're old and you've had a good life but nobody is sad that you died because it's about time."

"I'm not going to die."

"Everyone has to. It says so in scripture."

"Well, I don't have to like it."

"Sister Jasper died sitting up in church. That might be nice."

"Likely she got bored to death," Levi said, grinning.

"The worst way to go," she said, and they laughed together.

This simple wedding ceremony and reception at church

had been anything but boring, and if she were honest, she remembered that Sister Jasper had been smiling in her Sleep. Still, Levi had a way of making naughtiness seem all right, and she liked that about him. It was comfortable.

Coby, on the other hand—there he was helping Mother with the serving, doing what Rebecca herself should have been doing. Somehow, without saying a word, without even meaning to, he was always making her want to be better than she was. Well. She wouldn't look at him.

She smiled up at Levi.

He smiled down at her. "You still haven't come to see my horses," he said.

"Mother keeps me busy," she said.

Sister Fletcher had brought along Abigail the baby, who now began to wail.

"I shall go outside until that settles," Levi said with a smile, and he made his escape. She noticed that Radonna followed him out the door.

Coby came to collect her empty plate.

"I should be doing that," Rebecca said, just a bit resentfully.

Abigail continued to wail.

"Do you have opinions about babies, Coby?" she asked.

He swallowed his Adam's apple.

"Of course you want one," she said.

"I suppose I do," he said.

"It's just like you," she said.

Father and Mother gave Gideon gifts upon his wedding: five cows. Father and his sons would continue to work the operation together, but Gideon would have his own brand now, against the day he'd want to pass his spread on to his sons.

Such riches! Five cows! Furthermore, Philemon came with a dowry of sorts from her father.

All this gave Rebecca an idea.

When her father and brothers looked at a cow, they saw money. When she looked at a cow, she thought how brutal a fate it had, to eat nothing but grass all its life and then to end up on the plate. She had heard of a man named Mr. Godsall in Fort Macleod who had achieved small fame because he never ate meat and yet kept living, though people predicted he would die of it one day. She wished she might be so noble, but she was always hungry enough to eat anything, including cow.

Now she would look at cows like business.

She waited until after the excitement of Gideon's wedding had died down before she presented her idea to Father. She found him in the barn cleaning and scraping his horse's hooves.

"Father, I do love you."

"Thank you, Rebecca. What is it you want?"

"Father, when I marry, will you also give me gifts?"

"It is the custom."

"Then might I tell you what I would like?"

Father set down Blue's hind foot and stroked him from his back down to the other foot, which Blue politely raised. Father began cleaning the other hoof.

"And what would that be?"

"Five cows."

"Five cows? When you have found someone who will marry you, time enough for talk of wedding gifts."

"So you are saying, Father, that when I marry you will give me five cows?"

"Rebecca, Gideon did a man's work all these years..."

"I wouldn't ask for five cows. Only four."

"You will marry a man whose father will help him get started."

"Father, think about the hard work Mother does, awake before dawn, cooking and cleaning and working in the garden all day long, milking and caring for the chickens and pigs, sewing at night. Should I ask her if a woman's work is not worth three cows?"

Father gouged out a stubborn piece of gravel. He set down Blue's foot, and his implement.

"And do I not labor beside Mother in all things, Father? At least two cows' worth of labor?"

"You do, daughter. I have seen especially lately that you are a help to her." He stood up. "Very well. When you marry you shall have a cow, and a good one, too."

"Thank you, Father!" She threw her arms around him, and he patted her back, seeming glad to have the matter settled.

She stood back, beaming. "And now, Father, there is another matter."

He sighed and began to clean his tools wearily. "Say on, daughter."

"What if I don't get married?" There was the possibility that Radonna in her pink silk dress could capture Levi's heart. She was doing her very best.

"You will marry, daughter. You are as pretty and as clever as your mother when I met her."

"If you are so certain of my prospects, then, might I have my future wedding gift now? In advance of the happy day?"

He straightened and stood still, blinking at her, hands loose at his sides. Since Father was never still, it was alarming to see him so. She resisted the desire to take back what she had said.

"Please, Father? I must save so much money. Eggs and butter and even Abigail the pig will never be enough."

He filled his chest with air and let it out slowly. He shook his head and began to leave the barn.

"Rebecca, it is a fool's errand, and it would take more cows than one to earn the cost of that land. But you may have it."

Father might have been surprised at her good eye, for she chose a heifer out of the herd that was spare and deep-bodied. That kind of cow, she knew, consumed the most feed and made the best use of it. The percentage of butterfat in the milk, Mother had taught her, was influenced by many things: if the weather was particularly rainy or cold, if the cow had been worried by coyotes, or not gentled enough by her people. So Rebecca gentled her cow, and Father said he had never seen such coddling. When the cow had her first calf, she would make a beautiful milch cow. For now Rebecca was milking the family's cow, often Coby's cow, and, at times, and secretly, Sempel's cow. Her arms ached so much at night, sometimes, she could hardly sleep. But her money box got heavier. Every day she packed the butter into a twenty-five-pound tub down cellar, salting it well, and covering it carefully, ready to sell in town along with her eggs. Eventually she would add to it the money from the sale of her pig.

Still. Even still.

Father was right.

No matter how she added the numbers it would not be enough. She couldn't see how she could save enough money from butter before Coby's preemption deadline came up.

Coby was away again for a few days, so she took the wagon to tend his cow and chickens. As usual, she made a stop at the tor on the way home. God wasn't there, of course.

It had clouded over, and the tor was gray as a winter's moon. Nothing could be so lonely-looking, she thought, as a Sitting Rock with Nobody sitting on it, when it had once been Sat Upon.

She stared at the mountains.

They surprised her every time, those mountains, by being so hard to pack into her brain. Are you really that glorious? her brain wanted to ask.

If she couldn't somehow get the money for her land in time, she knew Coby would let her come to the tor. But what if he married? She didn't like the thought of him marrying—there was no one good enough for him, she was sure—he'd be better off as a bachelor. But knowing him, he would marry, and like as not his wife wouldn't want Rebecca riding all over her land. It would be even worse if Coby gave up his rights and Sempel stepped up to buy the land—it was a certainty that Sempel would never let her wander on the tor.

Rebecca knew it was more than just wanting to visit the tor. It was a yearning in her to hold on to something that had happened to her, to put her hands on those rocks and say, I own this rock, and I own that thing that happened to me. It is mine.

She could doubt her own eyes, but she had taken something away with her when she'd had her Sit. She had felt in that moment that living was just a thin floating thing like a cloud, a skim of dust on the river, the call of a wolf filling the air, striking the sky as if it were a glass bowl and ringing away forgotten. She could still feel it, if she tried. If that wasn't proof, she didn't know what was.

She couldn't give up. There had to be a way to have her land. God might have all manner of tricks up his omnipotent sleeves.

Brother Sempel

With fall came a rich, slantwise light, cool nights and hot days and skies full of geese flying away south. They called a warning as they flew in great windy arrows.

The men brought in the second hay crop—mowed it and raked it to dry and loaded it into the hay wagon to store in the barn. Rebecca helped when she wasn't helping Mother. The men were making sure the cattle would make it over the winter, and Rebecca and Mother would make sure the people would live, too.

In the cellar dark, potatoes and rutabagas and carrots and beets from Mother's garden slept in dusty bushel baskets. Heaped like treasure were hundred-pound bags of flour, oats, and rice that Father had bought after the cattle auction. Glass jars, of peas and pickles and saskatoons, that Rebecca had picked and preserved, shone like jewels on the shelves. There was sweet-sour chokecherry syrup for pancakes, and jars and jars of saskatoon jam. Mother had also bottled venison for days when the hunting might be poor. The mother pig was now hanging as hams from string in the shed beside the barn, along with the wheels of cheese and tubs of good salted butter and paper bags of dried beans.

Mother and Rebecca went down cellar together and

admired their stores. Animals could bear the cold, Mother said, but people could outsmart it.

They had been able to afford some other store-bought goods, too: Granite Wax Candles, Silverleaf Brand Pure Lard, Rogers Golden Syrup, and Christie Brown and Company First Prize Golden Graham Wafers. Winter wasn't quite as fearsome if you had a box of graham wafers. Philemon had likewise laid away as many foodstuffs as she could in such a short time in her own cellar.

The men had made several trips to the timber, mostly for pine and aspen. They cut the trees into stove lengths with a crosscut saw and stacked the wood against the back of the houses for winter. They would work until they were as ready for winter as they could be. From the mountains you could see Montana to the south, and British Columbia to the west: you couldn't see the North Pole to the north, but come winter, you would feel it right enough.

The days were getting shorter, and it wouldn't be long before it was dark long into the morning and dark again by late afternoon, the kind of dark that made you forget a blue sky.

Until it became impossible, the family would go to church each Sunday. Rebecca sat in the wagon backward to watch the mountains as they drove there. The wind blew the silence around. Sometimes Rebecca found the Sabbath too solemn and the silence too oppressive, but this day, with the wind running in the fields, she didn't mind. The mountains glowed as if they'd swallowed the moon. It was one of those days that made you take the weather's tantrums in benign acceptance in the hope of another day like this.

Mother greeted and shook hands with people as they made their way into the meetinghouse. Gideon and Philemon took their own selves to church now, and Mother greeted them like they were real people and not her very own children.

"I am missing your wife again today," Mother said quietly to Brother Sempel.

Brother Sempel said gruffly, "She hasn't been feeling well. She'll feel better soon. You needn't stop by."

"Might I help...? She's fond of my dinner rolls..."

Brother Sempel stuck out his chest and lifted his chin.

"She wouldn't want you. She told me to tell you."

"I see," Mother said.

Brother Sempel walked away, and Mother studied the air where he'd been standing.

Mother and her daughter-in-law exchanged a long look and went silently into the church.

Before the service began, Rebecca slipped around the corner of the church building to find Father smoking again.

"Our sins shall be shouted from the rooftops," Father said, putting out his cigarette against the log wall. He looked at her looking at him and said, "The good Lord gives us weakness to keep us humble." She took his hand and they went in together.

After services, Brother Card asked everyone to stay for a special meeting. It took people a while to settle—they needed to stand and shift about and chat after being reminded of their sins for an hour. But at last they were seated and still and turned their attention to Brother Card at the podium.

"I don't need to tell you that we need more access to water if we're to make better use of the land, and open it up for more of our people," he said. "As you know, I've been meeting with Mr. Magrath, who represents the interests of Elliott Galt, who has land grants he can't get rid of without a canal to lure buyers. We have finally settled on a plan. The deal is this: our people construct the canal—he knows we are the only ones with the expertise—and he will pay us for our labors, half in land and half in cash."

There was a murmur of approval.

"How much land is Magrath talking about?" Father asked.

"Ten thousand acres. For fifty-five miles of canal. I had to promise that our people will have no say in things—no place of leadership on the project. Our job is to build the canal. He wants to avoid an uproar from those not of our faith."

"But it's our people," said Brother Fletcher, "who will do the work. And we'll need help from the folks from Utah willing to settle here. We won't have enough workers without them."

"That's true," Brother Card said, smiling. "And just in time, for there's a land shortage in Utah these days."

"The protesters in Lethbridge won't like that."

"They'll like it when they see we have watered a land once thought too dry for any use to anyone. Are we going to do this?"

Brother Card let the men talk among themselves for a time, but everyone knew the canal was necessary for opening up the land for settlement and for protection from drought. When finally he asked, "All in favor?" every arm was raised.

Rebecca raised hers especially high. Here was the miracle she'd been praying for. All those men working on the canal come early spring would need to be fed. They would be looking for women for the cook crew. And she would be one of those women.

On the way home from church, nobody could speak of anything but the canal. Except Ammon, who talked only of LaRue. Rebecca said, "You know she is the most perfect of human beings."

"She is that," Ammon said, not even pretending to misunderstand her.

"You know you don't deserve her."

"I know it."

"Tell me you mean it."

"I mean it, Rebecca. I mean it forever. I'm going to marry her forever."

"Have you asked her father's permission?"

"I have, but he wants us to wait, to be sure. He says her brothers need her at home. He says when I have the house ready, maybe by then . . ."

"Well, your house is all but ready, so it sounds hopeful."

He nodded.

Since LaRue started saying nice things about Ammon, Rebecca had begun to see him differently. She saw how he bore up under the teasing of his older brothers. She saw how he tried hard to rise to Father's expectations. He went as often as he could courting to LaRue now, though Sister Fletcher made sure the courting candle was the shortest she could find. When the candle went out, the courting was done for the evening. Zach, too, was going out in the evenings sometimes, though he never said where he was going. He always looked worried—whoever it was he was seeing was not making it easy on him, Rebecca decided.

Absorbed in thought as she was, she didn't notice when the wagon had veered away from the direction of home, Father looking none too pleased, and Mother looking resolute.

"Where are we going?" Rebecca asked.

"The Sempels', looks like," Ammon said.

When they pulled into the yard, Brother Sempel came out of his house and slammed the door.

"Thought for sure I said visitors weren't wanted."

"We don't mean to intrude—" Mother began.

"But you have done so," Sempel said.

"I just wanted to invite Sister Sempel to a quilting bee this Friday," Mother said.

"I'll tell her. Now be on your way."

He spoke to Mother in a tone Rebecca had never heard anyone use toward Mother. She wondered how Father was bearing it, and now she saw that he wasn't.

"I'll ask you to speak to my wife with respect," Father said in a low, growling voice.

Father flicked his team, and the wagon turned about.

Supper was the usual Sunday fare of baked beans and yesterday's bread, but Mother was quiet and solemn, as if she'd never left church.

Father tried to cheer Mother up with talk of the canal and all it implied, and she seemed to try.

It hadn't occurred to Rebecca before that Mother could be sad. It came to her now as a revelation, though not of the spiritual kind. It was as if her eyes were opened — Mother could not fix everything, including whatever was wrong with Sister Sempel.

This terrible feeling settled on Rebecca for days and weeks as the world seemed to show her that it was a dark and dangerous place now that Mother was sad. Rebecca felt she was Eve, finding herself in a cold and dreary world: a cow struck by lightning, a woman giving birth to a twelve-pound baby, a foot-long tapeworm sliding out of Audran Campbell's nose while he was asleep.

Gideon defingered himself while fencing. He picked up the bit of finger and rode home without a word to anyone. Philemon cut some skin off the bit of separated finger and stitched the slip of skin over the stump like a little cap, using her finest stitches. After, she had to go to bed for the rest of the day, but Gideon went back to work with a bandaged hand.

Worst of all, a young boy wandered into the timber while his father was cutting trees and was never seen again. The boy's family packed up their goods and their sorrow and moved away south.

Sempel's cow had come infrequently at first, but lately more frequently. Rebecca suspected it liked her tender hands. One morning when she was dwelling on the darkening days and the dark news, Sempel's cow again wandered into their barn to munch on their hay. Rebecca was so preoccupied that she forgot to take only some, and she milked that spotty cow vigorously until there was nothing left. She felt bad for a moment, and then she felt fine.

Later that afternoon Brother Sempel showed up at the Leavitts' door carrying an empty milk pail. Beside him was Coby.

"Brother Sempel," Mother said politely. "How is your good wife?" She did not invite them in.

"Well enough," Sempel grunted.

"Coby," Mother said with a shining smile.

"Brother Sempel came to me with his problem first," Coby said, "and as I was unable to help him with it, he said he would go to you next. I thought I'd come along."

"What is the problem?" Father said, coming up behind Mother. Zach and Ammon were behind him. Brother Sempel looked so angry that Rebecca felt glad of Coby standing before her, and her great big brothers standing behind Father.

Brother Sempel said, "My milch cow has been giving us barely enough milk for our own use for some time now. At first my wife said it must be sick. But now I know that somebody has been stealing."

Father stared at the bucket.

"Stealing your bucket?"

"Not my bucket. What goes into the bucket. Milk, in other words. You can see my bucket is milkless, Brother Leavitt. As was my milch cow, when she came home today."

"Your cows go home?" Ammon said pertly.

Brother Sempel gave him a sour look, and Coby hid a smile.

"Webster here swears he isn't milking my cow and knows nothing about it, and so the only other culprit could be you, living close by as you do."

Mother tipped her head and her eyes turned slowly to Rebecca as if she were trying to puzzle something out.

Father said, "You must be in error, sir, for I have never in my life taken what isn't mine."

Brother Sempel stood his ground. "I've come for apology and compensation."

Rebecca wondered briefly if it would be okay to Love the World Minus One. But that would be like living in a world where one candy apple was always an onion, and you could never be too sure about anything.

"Rebecca is the one who does the milking," Father said. "Daughter, would you know anything about this?"

Studying the situation, and coming to the conclusion that the only one who could get her out of this trouble was God, she decided upon the stratagem of telling the truth.

"I do, Father," she said. Why did all her good ideas shrivel under the scrutiny of her parents? "The Sempels' cow eats our grass, and the milch cow has also been in our barn eating our hay. I tried to get it out, but it wouldn't understand English, so I...I suppose I thought, milk for hay. It seemed only fair."

Father and Mother and her brothers and Coby and Brother Sempel: they all looked at her for a long moment.

"Milk for hay," Father repeated.

He seemed to stew over those words for a time, as if he were searching in his mind the scripture that might make this seem wrong. But there must not have been one, for finally he turned to Brother Sempel, open-faced and benevolent.

"Milk for hay. A fair arrangement, wouldn't you say, Brother Sempel? Your cows have been eating our grass and our hay. We have been taking milk in payment."

Brother Sempel's mustache shifted from side to side, and he glowered at Rebecca.

"You are a bad girl," he said to Rebecca. "If I were your father, you'd get a whipping."

Father and her brothers—even Coby—seemed to fill their chests with air.

"Her mother and I take credit for the way she's turned out," Father said. "And now it's time you were going."

"I see I shall have to find a way to keep my bossies at home," Sempel said.

Father nodded. "Pray about it, Brother Sempel," he said soberly. "Only pray, and a way will be provided."

Brother Sempel turned and stomped off.

Rebecca and Father stepped onto the porch to watch him leave.

"I'll tell you what I think," Sempel said to them before he rode away. "I think if this place ain't hell, you sure enough can see it from here."

Now it was time to face Father's justice for what she'd done to Brother Sempel. Rebecca wondered if Mother would rescue her, but Mother had disappeared inside the house, and her brothers and Coby headed out to the barn. It was just her and Father.

"I'm sorry—" she said, though if she were honest she was mostly just sorry that she'd have less butter money now.

He placed his hand gently on her shoulder.

"Daughter," he said wearily, "there's the blood of Solomon in you."

She thought a moment. "Wasn't Solomon the king who would have had to marry every two weeks his entire life to have wedded all his wives?"

Father sighed. He patted her shoulder. "Just be good," he said.

BLIZZARD

Winter announced itself in November with a blizzard. Mother saw the long, low line of black clouds at the horizon—sure sign of a coming blizzard—through her kitchen window. She tore off her apron.

"Come, Rebecca! We've got to make sure the animals made it to the barn..."

Rebecca ran with Mother to gather the horses in, but the horses had known about the storm long before. They and the pigs and chickens and the milch cow were huddled in the warm barn. The Cat Named Dog, even knowing the barn belonged to her, had let them in without complaining. The beef cattle would stay out in the storm, huddled together behind the wood-slab windbreak the men had built.

After quickly making sure the animals had feed and water enough for a few days, and a little blue block of salt, she and Mother tied a strong rope between the barn and the house, and reached the house just as the wind began to bluster and blow and as the clouds began to black out the sky to the north. Philemon was in the house when they got back.

"Gideon told me to come here whenever there may be a blizzard and he'll meet me here. He doesn't want me to be alone because of—"

She stopped, but her hands went to her belly.

Mother understood immediately and smiled with joy. It took Rebecca a little longer to figure out that Gideon didn't want Philemon alone in her house during a blizzard because of a *baby*.

Mother hugged Philemon and they began cooking for the men, who would surely be heading for home.

Suddenly Mother stopped.

"Coby," she said, and she sat down.

"Coby?" Rebecca said.

"I — I invited him for supper, but he said he had to go to his south field first... What if he got caught?"

"He'll be all right, Mother," Rebecca said. She said it like a prayer, like it could make everything all right by saying it.

"Yes," Mother said. "He would go home. He wouldn't take chances."

"What's taking the men so long?" Philemon asked, staring out the window, her hands folded tightly at her waist. "There! There they come."

The women watched as the men raced the storm to the barn and disappeared inside. They were still in the barn when the storm hit, the house instantly like an ark in a wild prairie sea. The snow came screaming at the door and windows, thundering at the north side of the house. Utah had had blizzards, of course, but not so cold and not so relentless and vicious as the ones here in the Territories. Mother instructed Rebecca to hang quilts at the windows so the icy air wouldn't seep in, and in case the wind broke the glass.

They finished making supper. That was what they always did when there was nothing else to be done: cook. Against the storm, they would eat, and eat well, as if to celebrate the storm. This was what the hoarding had been for.

At last the door banged opened and the men stomped in, covered in snow and looking like ghosts, and the snow roared in after them. They had found their way with the rope, for they could not see their hands before their eyes. Philemon and Gideon embraced.

Rebecca stood at the door and looked into the blind white of the blizzard.

"Close the door, Rebecca," Ammon said.

"Coby was going to come," she said.

That stopped Ammon. "He'll be all right," he said after a moment.

They ate, but distractedly, while the wind wailed at the windows and the chimney, wanting to be let in. Ammon played the mouth organ, but the happy songs felt wrong, and the sad songs felt too sad.

Rebecca listened for a knock at the door, listened with all her might, but she could hear nothing but the wailing and bellowing of the wind, blowing as if it wanted to thrash the life out of anything upright.

"Wind alone, or cold alone, or snow alone, a man can live through," Zach said. "But God help the man who gets caught out in all three at once."

Rebecca stood up. She stood as if she were going to say something, shout something, but she had no idea what that might be, or why she was standing, so she sat down again.

After a time, Mother said, "Children, when I die, bury me on the lee side of the cemetery, please, or I'll come haunt you."

Rebecca replied in a monotone voice that a ghost, in these winds, wouldn't make it home, but would be blown to Britain before it had a chance to haunt. Father said God made sure spirits were kept tidily on their own side of the veil, just as mortals were on their side. Rebecca said she had heard whisperings of instances when mortals had seen the spirit world, and she knew of her own experience that things were not so tidy and without leaks as most people suspected. Father said that was enough of that kind of talk as they had enough to worry about in this life to keep them busy. All this above the screaming storm.

Her brothers revived old stories they had heard of people who got caught in a winter storm and somehow survived it. One man huddled at the side of his horse who lay beside him in the snow, and when the storm died, so, too, did the horse, though the man lived. He gave his horse a proper burial and a tombstone. Another man tipped his wagon upside down and huddled beneath it until the storm blew itself into exhaustion. Still another, Brother Stonewell, was returning home with his wagon and team when a blizzard caught him out. He couldn't see a thing, so he gave the horses their lead. Suddenly they stopped cold, and nothing he could do would persuade them to move another inch. He got down from the wagon to see what was the trouble, and there before his eyes was a barn door, his very own barn door. The horses had brought him home and saved his life.

Somehow none of the stories made anyone feel any better.

Father said they would go to Coby's first thing in the morning, assuming the blizzard had blown itself out, and it was time for family prayer and bed.

"I will wait up a little longer, Mother," Rebecca said.

"I won't let you stay up alone," Mother said.

So Rebecca, knowing Mother must be up early as always to cook breakfast, went to bed and prayed herself to sleep.

Overnight the blizzard tired itself out, though it raged in her dreams. By morning, everything was still and the world was white and cold.

The men were already eating breakfast when she came out of her room. "You're going to make sure Coby is okay?"

Father nodded but didn't stop eating.

"I'm coming," Rebecca said.

Father looked sharply at her, but Mother said, "You may."

Rebecca quickly ate, then bundled up a loaf of fresh bread and some leftovers. Coby would be hungry, she said to Mother, and she went with the men to the barn for the horses.

Before they got to Coby's house, they saw there was no smoke coming from the chimney. Rebecca had never before wished for something so ordinary as to see a slip of smoke coming from a chimney.

"You get a fire going, Rebecca," Father said. "We'll go looking."

Rebecca got the fire going in the cookstove. She could do that. She could do that without thinking.

Once the fire was blazing, she could clean. She could do that. She could do anything but sit there and wait.

She swept and made the bed, Coby's bed. She made it and smoothed it out. The quilt was ragged and thin, but the bed was made. She washed his one poor cup and one poor plate and one poor fork and knife. She organized the things on the shelves and hung some clothes on pegs and trimmed the lantern wicks. She went to the water hole, cracked the ice, and hauled a bucket of water back. She did all this desperately, as if he would walk in the door any moment.

And then he did.

He stood in the doorway, in only a light jacket, covered in straw, and rocked on his feet.

"Are you real?" he said.

He sagged, and she helped him to his bed, took off his boots, checked his fingers and toes, which were all there and not frostbitten, and covered him with his ragged quilt.

"I shall make you a new quilt if you will live," she said.

His eyes were closed and he was groggy, but he was speaking to her, telling her in fits and starts what had happened. She warmed water and made him drink.

He had been on foot in his south field when the storm struck. He knew he had a haystack between himself and the house, but, though he knew where the haystack was, he didn't know where he was.

"I prayed as I've never prayed, Rebecca... and I walked right into that haystack... right into it... I burrowed in, and found my two pigs had burrowed in first... Do you know how warm a pig is, Rebecca?"

He was falling asleep even as he spoke.

She tucked the quilt around him.

"Sleep, and when you wake up, you shall have whatever you like," she said, meaning something to eat. She almost brushed his hair from his eyes, and then drew her hand back.

"I would like your company," he said, half dreaming.

"You shall have it," she said, "and with a little salt, too."

Father and her brothers returned to Coby's house, having found no trace of him out in the fields, and thanked the Lord in whispers when they found Coby sleeping peacefully, breathing deeply. Rebecca told them the story of how he had survived.

"The pigs kept him from freezing but he hasn't slept. I'll heat the leftovers for when he wakes up."

Father nodded.

When they were gone, she looked around the house at her leisure. She saw the scriptures on a little table by his bed, and his shaving gear on the wash table, as if he were a man and not this boy who'd slept with his clever pigs all night. There was a neat little pile of letters from home on the dresser, and an arrowhead.

She'd found that arrowhead when they'd first arrived and given it to him.

She got busy with the leftovers.

Two hours later Coby woke up and sat up slowly. He looked around at his little log house, swept and tidy, the fire snapping, a meal laid out on the small table, and Rebecca sitting at the foot of the bed.

"There you are," she said.

"I thought for a moment I had died and this was heaven."

"This would be your heaven?" she asked. "You have low expectations."

She was suddenly keenly aware that she was sitting on the bed of a bachelor without any chaperone. It was only Coby, after all, but—

She stood up slowly.

"I told Father I'd stay until you were awake."

"Thank you, Reb," he said. He said it softly, as if he were saying something else, something she couldn't or wouldn't understand.

"Don't thank me. You've been given a miracle, Coby Webster. You'll have to be a better man now. That's what happens when you get a miracle. It's not always an easy thing."

She knew that better than anybody. Coby, she realized, could hardly be a better man than he already was. But she—she had a long ways to go, and here she was telling him how to be.

He nodded, not taking his eyes off her.

"I've warmed up some food for you, and I'll cut the bread before I go. I know you like the crusts, so you shall have all three."

"Three? Aren't there only two heels to a loaf?"

She cut each end, and then sliced off the top.

"Three crusts," she said.

"I shall never doubt you again," he said.

"Mother suffered last night," she said, unable to say that she had hardly slept herself.

"I'm sorry. I misjudged how fast a storm would gallop across the prairie."

"Yes," she said. "Well."

She put on her coat and fled.

Later Coby came to the house to thank Father and her brothers for looking for him. He found Rebecca working on a new quilt for him, made of all the scraps of her brothers' worn-out shirts and britches.

"It will be ugly," she said, "as all my quilts are ugly. But it will keep you warmer than that sorry excuse for a quilt you have."

He said thank you, and this time when he said it, all her family looked at him as if he had said something momentous. Rebecca thought of Radonna's ten stitches to the inch and tried to make her stitches smaller. Coby deserved at least eight. Or nine. She'd vowed again and again the night before that she'd be good forever if only Coby would be all right, and there he was—all right—and there she was, same as she'd always been.

ENDLESS WINTER, 1891

Winter went on,
and winter went on.

Each morning they must build up the fires and thaw out the middle of the house. The corners of the house stayed frosted all through winter. Three meals a day had to be cooked in the brittle-cold house, but at least the more they cooked, the warmer the kitchen became. The men must venture into the snow to bring hay out to the range so the cattle wouldn't starve. Rebecca went, too, when Mother could spare her.

Rebecca kept her spirits up through sheer stubborn will and insisted on others doing the same.

When Zach fretted about the blizzard winds, Rebecca tried to cheer him, "But Zach, if the wind stopped blowing all the cows would topple over." When he smiled, she counted it a triumph.

"I heard down in Fort Keogh, Montana, it snowed snowflakes fifteen inches wide," Ammon said at dinner one blizzardy night.

Rebecca said proudly, "If there's a snowflake that big in Montana, there's one twice that size here."

"I won't disagree with you," Ammon replied. Which Rebecca found notable.

"Perhaps a Chinook will blow in," Mother said. A Chinook wind meant a bitterly cold January morning could become a shirtsleeve afternoon. But though they saw clouds forming a Chinook arch in the sky a time or two, the wind did little more than blow the cold around more fiercely.

Why did she love this place? Blizzards forcing them into hiding like gophers, the constant work against starvation, the endless wind that scoured out their ears. Why would she love such a place, this place that tried its best to kill you every day, and very nearly did kill Coby? Just because of heartbreaking mountains and Chinook winds that came smelling of apples and the sea? She could go away, but she'd only be a ghost anywhere else, without this land around her, with these mountains reminding her every day just what Mother Earth could do if she set her mind to it. That, as much as anything, made her want her land, and every day she dreamed of it.

Rebecca worried about the cows. She worried about the spindly-legged deer and where they hid when the storms struck. She was always surprised to see them reappear after a storm, still with their twiggy legs attached and not frozen off. But she said nothing of her worries and reminded everyone not to complain and worked on her quilt for Coby.

Winter in February all but froze the sun out of the sky. The mountains became great walls of snow, the prairie a vast white expanse, dangerous and bleak. It took faith to believe anything could come out of it alive ever again.

Down cellar, the bags of oats and rice looked loose and the bottled goods were beginning to look lonely on the shelves. The cheeses were almost gone, and only the ugliest rutabagas remained. The potatoes that dared to grow eyes were bagged for spring planting, if spring would ever come.

Rebecca pressed her thumb onto the window frost until it melted. Then she pressed petals around the thumbprint and made a daisy. A daisy. Surely there would never be such a thing again. Meal time staples were bread and oatmeal—the milch cow had dried up, the chickens weren't laying, and nothing was left of the mama pig but the sausage. Then one of Father's cows went down on an ice glare, all four feet in different directions, tearing muscles and ligaments. It had to be slaughtered for it would never stand again. That meant beef for supper until spring. Father said he hated to eat his profits, and Mother said eating was what profits were for and no venison made as delicious a roast as one of their own cows.

Winter went on and on.

Rebecca was forced to admire Radonna for making the most of winter, for she gathered the young people at her house, when the weather allowed, for taffy pulls and dramatics and charades and sleigh rides. She had once said she'd go to Utah as soon as she could get there, but Rebecca had to admit that she made the best of things, and she did it with grace. Furthermore, she always invited Rebecca, so Rebecca persuaded herself that Radonna didn't like Levi as much as she had thought she did.

From a brother in Utah they received a crate of old copies of *The Deseret News* and *Woman's Exponent*, which made the dark evenings more bearable. Father read about a robber named Butch Cassidy, who was making a name for himself.

"Will Butch Cassidy go to heaven, seeing he's one of our own?" Rebecca asked.

"Only if he wants to. All God's children go to heaven if they want to."

"But then why can't I rob a bank if God loves everyone the same?"

"Because before you met with God's mercy, you would have to meet with my justice, and you wouldn't want that."

"No, Father," she said, "I would not."

Coby came for supper when he could, and it was always better when he was there. Sometimes, though, the memory of sitting with him on his bed would come in the middle of comfortable conversations, and she would feel awkward and strange with him.

Occasionally Levi dropped in on long evenings, at times when Coby was there. And tonight was one of those nights.

"I met up with Ammon on his way to visit LaRue, and thought I'd come eat his share," Levi said.

Mother welcomed him warmly. Philemon and Gideon had come, too, so there would be eight for supper.

Coby was less talkative and cheerful, now that Levi had come.

"Won't Radonna miss you tonight?" Coby asked.

"She never lacks for friends," Levi said.

Rebecca helped Mother get the dinner on the table, but tried to hear what the men were talking about as she did so.

Father asked for Levi's expertise on horses. To think that anyone knew anything that Father didn't was impressive to Rebecca, and she hoped her admiration for Levi wasn't obvious to her family.

Over dinner, Coby aired his opinion in favor of protecting their part of the Rocky Mountains from hunters by making it a park reserve, just like Banff.

Rebecca said to Levi, as if to explain, "Coby doesn't hunt. He says the wild things don't ask anything of us and work all their days to survive, so it seems unfair to add to their troubles." She didn't know why she was saying this when Coby was sitting right there and could speak for himself.

"Coby has his opinions," Levi said.

"They killed off all the elk," Coby said. "Easterners did. Every single elk they could find, and you know why? To make jewelry of their eyeteeth. Left their carcasses lying there with just their eyeteeth gone."

"It's a shame," Father said.

"But they'll come back," Coby said. "There are elk in those mountains, I bet, hiding in places where men can't go. You'll see them again."

"I'm afraid they've gone the way of the buffalo," Levi said. "Maybe just as well. A herd of hungry elk can raze a man's haystack in a single winter's night."

"They're hungry because people let their cattle eat down the elk's winter range all summer long," said Coby.

Father and her brothers were looking from Coby to Levi as if bewildered as to how the conversation had turned from friendly to tense.

"I say the good Lord gave us dominion, and he also gave us guns," Levi said. "One plus one equals two."

Rebecca thought about that. She admired that Levi had called the Lord good, but she had to admit that she didn't really understand his arithmetic. She waited for Coby to speak, but he did not.

"Coby says guns are the product of a fallen world," she said. "He says sometimes we're cruel to Mother Nature." She realized that at some point she had stopped speaking for Coby and was speaking for herself.

Mother smiled, though Rebecca did not know why. Did she agree? She who could fell a prairie chicken on the first shot?

Levi said, "I suppose we are sometimes cruel to Mother Nature. But she was first cruel to us."

Rebecca had no answer for that, with bitter winter on the other side of the door. It seemed neither did Coby, who was looking at her with a wondering look, though she couldn't imagine why.

Just as they were finishing dinner, Ammon found his way home. Mother fussed over him a bit, but he said he was fine and had eaten at LaRue's.

Rebecca, Mother, and Philemon cleared the dishes and got out their sewing. It seemed everyone had run out of things to talk about, when there came a knock.

"We are popular this night," Father said, rising to get the door.

He opened it and a gust of icy air blew in Kootenai Brown.

"Mr. Brown! Come in, come in!" Mother said.

"Please, let me take your coat," Father said.

"Thank you," Kootenai said.

Father hung his fur coat and white Stetson on the

antlers, and Mother busied herself warming milk and slicing bread. Her brothers set Kootenai in the best chair and the men gathered their chairs about him.

"Please don't fuss yourself over me," Kootenai said.

"We shall always fuss over you. How do you come to be here this night, Kootenai?" Father sat on the edge of his chair as if royalty had come to visit, and he was ready to provide for his every whim.

"Thank you, ma'am," Kootenai said, taking the milk and bread and butter from Mother.

"You will stay the night, Mr. Brown, of course," she said.

"I'm grateful for the offer, but I must get back, and I didn't come to be social. I came to tell you about your cattle—yours and some of yours, too, Coby, if I remember your brands."

"Our cattle?" Father and Coby said at the same time.

"The wind has driven 'bout forty head of them into the hills, and they're trapped by snowdrifts. I tried to get in there and drive them out, but they fear the deep snow more than they fear man."

Rebecca knew this was bad. Very bad. The cattle would starve and freeze and die, trapped in the drifts like that.

The men talked at length in solemn voices about exactly where the cattle were, and what could be done to rescue them. None of their plans had a happy ending.

At last Kootenai stood. "Well, I leave you to it. I thank you for the bit of fire and bread."

Everyone stood. Mother gave Kootenai a jar of preserves to take home to Mrs. Brown. Father got down

Kootenai's Stetson from the antlers, his muffler, and his coat, and he was gone into the cold dark.

After a silence, Zach said, "That's us, starving and freezing in the drifts, too, if it comes down to it. Our ranch can't survive so great a loss."

"It's true, this would surely ruin us," Gideon said.

"What will we do?" Ammon asked.

Father shook his head and said nothing.

Zach said, "That's it, then. The cows are done for. That's all our profit for this year and next, too. They're done for, and so are we."

"Please not to go crawling into your own grave just yet," Rebecca said. "Levi is a man of solutions. You have an idea, don't you, Levi?"

"I wish I did," he said.

Coby cleared his throat. "I might have an idea."

She looked at him skeptically.

"What's the one critter who isn't afraid of the deep snow?" Coby asked.

The men studied him and said nothing.

"A Blackfoot pony," said Coby.

"Yes," Levi said. "That is true."

Coby was thinking as he talked. "We can round up my ponies, herd them right up to the cattle, they stomp down the drifts, we lead the cattle out."

A long silence, and then Father said, "Outrageous idea, but it might work. Coby, stay the night, and we'll get to it in the morning."

Levi said, "I'll help."

So he stayed the night, too.

Mother and Philemon and Rebecca were up early making an enormous breakfast. The men ate, and as soon as the skies began to lighten, they geared up.

"I want to go," Rebecca said.

Father said, "You stay. Mother could use your help. We'll all be back hungry, no matter how it ends."

"It's cold for a young lady," Levi said.

"That's no young lady—that's Rebecca. Let her come," Coby said.

Father looked at him—looked up at him, actually—and seemed only then to notice that Coby was taller than him.

"Well," Father said. "You'd best get in your mother's britches, then, Rebecca." As if the last thing he wanted now was an argument with his daughter.

Rebecca had never seen her mother wear her britches, but she knew where they were, folded in her wooden chest, laid away when her boys got big enough to be all the help Father needed.

The sun was sharp in the eye, a small white sun that gave no warmth but glittered up the snow in a way that was at first pretty, and soon blinding.

Rebecca had dressed in every warm thing Mother could find, but they hadn't ridden long before she was miserable. She thought of the cows starving in the drifts, and she made herself and her horse be heat enough. Coby rode at her side.

In the brutal cold they headed to Coby's to round up the ponies and herd them toward the place where Kootenai had seen the trapped cattle. The hot breath of horses, ponies, and people made small blue clouds in the cold. The men's mustaches and beards grew feathers of frost. Rebecca's feet were entirely numb. They rode without complaint. To complain would have made it unbearable. They rode toward the mountains, where the trees cracked and groaned in the cold.

It was a good long time getting there, but at last they could hear the bawling of the cows, and the ponies went more quickly, as if they knew their task. Coby, on his pony, led them on, and, bravely, the rest ploughed into the drifts. Behind them the people cheered them on with frozen faces and mouths. The ponies grunted and whinnied, and as one they pushed forward, up to their chests in the drifts, rearing up and coming down to stamp the deepest parts. At one point they seemed to tire, but Coby and the men encouraged them, and they finished the job.

They trampled the snow all the way to the cattle, and, as soon as the ponies turned about for home, the cows followed them out, bellowing, indignant, starving, exhausted.

They herded the cattle—two riders for the swing, two for the flank, and Coby and Rebecca in the drag, chasing the strays. Levi, riding magnificently, rode every position where he was needed. The ponies got ahead and would get home well enough on their own, Coby said.

Once the cows met up with the rest of the herd, they found the hay that the men had brought the day before. Among their fellows they would be fine now and Coby would collect his strays later.

"Have you saved the day?" Mother said when they all came into the house.

"Yes, and the cows, too, chickens that they are," Rebecca said. "I won't go out into the winter for the rest of my life."

Rebecca couldn't help with the meal, for her fingers and toes were so cold and numb. Mother and Philemon served up hot crusty buns with white butter melted in their hearts, fried mashed potatoes, sausages, and some of the last of Mother's precious preserves. Rebecca was served as if she were one of the men. The men ate a plateful of potatoes, and then helped themselves from the other dishes, and then had more potatoes. At the end of the meal, when she was given hot chocolate, Rebecca began to feel as if she might be warm again someday.

Levi warmly complimented the cooks. To Rebecca he said, "You were something, today."

"That's just the way she always is," Coby said to him.

Rebecca didn't know which one of them had made her happier. All she knew was that, let winter try its best, they would all still be here come spring.

CHINOOK

One day, when it seemed to Rebecca that it had been winter her entire life, she woke to the sound of the wind blowing down out of the mountains and water pouring off the roof and into the rain barrel.

She sat up straight in bed.

Chinook!

Rebecca in her nightdress threw open the door and stood on the porch. The wind tumbled wild down the mountains, and was blowing winter to kingdom come.

"Chinook!" she cried to no one.

Yesterday the world had been a frozen sheet, stiff on the line, the sky a wash of blueing. This morning the world was a warm patchwork quilt. She ran a little way into the yard. The horses danced in the Vicary field, a flock of Canada geese flew overhead, coming home.

She let the wind blow her nightdress between her legs, and finally let it push her back into the house to dress and help Mother fry potatoes. Mother sang while she cooked, and everyone was taking a certain pride from having got through another winter with all their fingers and toes still stuck on. Another year, and they had not winter-killed.

"Work will begin in earnest on the canal now," Zach said.

"I want to hire on," Ammon said.

"I can't spare you yet," Father said. "We've got roundup and branding first."

"But can you spare me, Mother?" Rebecca asked. "I wish to be a cook for the canal crew."

"No," Father said.

"Yes," Mother said over him. Rebecca had never in her life heard Mother speak over Father. "You can apply for the job right after the spring cleaning. If I need other help after that, Philemon is here so often, I know I can depend on her."

Mother and Rebecca began spring cleaning. Mother demanded cleanliness all times of the year, often saying that soap was the great civilizing invention. At all times of the year, everything had its place, and if one left something thoughtlessly on the table or counter where it didn't belong, one ran the risk of never seeing it again. But spring cleaning meant the carpets would be untacked, old straw padding swept out, the floors washed with lye soap until they were skinned of color and gave up the ghost. New rag rugs she and Mother had worked on all winter would be stretched and tacked down. Quilts were washed and hung in the bleaching sun. Cupboards were scoured, the windows and pictures and cookstove polished. If everyday housework was an obligation to goodness, spring cleaning was a moral triumph.

But as soon as spring cleaning was done, Rebecca went to the muster point to apply for a job.

"Can you cook, miss?" the man asked.

"I can peel potatoes faster than my mother," Rebecca said.

"Can you work, though? You've got to be tough for this job."

"I have three older brothers at home, and I've survived it."

That made him think. "You're hired," he said. "You can call me Cookie."

Ammon, once roundup was done, was hired on a team producing a million feet of lumber for sluiceways and gates. Coby quit hauling freight and got part-time work on the same team, working for cash only. Zach and Gideon would watch over his stock when he was away. Levi also joined the crew and hired a man to care for his spread, partly from his wages and partly in horseflesh.

LaRue, hearing that Ammon was going to be working on the canal, suddenly decided that she could not be without Rebecca for all that time and signed up to cook, too. LaRue worried how her mother would manage the boys without her, but she would use part of her wages to pay for a hired girl to come in some days. Their friends Minnie and Lyla would also be part of the cook crew. Work would stop on Saturday afternoon so everyone could go home and be ready for church on Sunday.

Before Rebecca and Ammon began work on the canal, Zach revealed his secret love by bringing her home to Mother and Father and announcing to the family that they were engaged. The mystery woman was Florence Andreeson.

Rebecca could not believe her eyes. She held out her hand to Florence to shake it.

"You're marrying my brother?" she asked Florence.

"We are meant," Florence said in a matter-of-fact way, as if she were reading a list of goods, as if this declaration didn't beg ridicule, even of the most affectionate kind. Rebecca had no desire to ridicule it. It suddenly seemed like the most sensible thing in the world to say, and she hoped she might say it one day. Of someone.

"But—what a secret!" Rebecca said.

"I kept it a secret because I wasn't sure she'd have me," Zach said.

Florence was almost as tall as Zach and looked people over with comfortable acceptance, which Rebecca knew could only be done by a person who comfortably accepted herself.

Rebecca sat at the table with Florence and stared unabashedly. Zach engaged, and to such an extraordinary creature! It seemed impossible that anyone like Florence could love her brother. But then, LaRue had set her heart upon Ammon, and Gideon had Philemon, and now Zach had gone and got Florence.

Florence was considering Rebecca at the same time. Finally she said, "I hear we are sisters in suffrage."

Rebecca hadn't known she was until that moment, but now she knew.

"Yes," she said. "Will it ever happen?"

"Utah was among the first States to give women the vote. Others will follow. A good idea can't be stopped."

"But here in Canada?"

"I have high hopes."

"Hard to hope, considering we are not persons."

"Brother Card's wife, Zina, is acquainted with Susan

Anthony and Matilda Gage," Florence said. "She will do her part."

"She is?" Rebecca looked around to see if Mother had heard. She must have, but she didn't give any sign. "Some women will think it unfeminine of her to know them."

Florence said, "As soon as we start pitting woman against woman, creating a standard by which we must be measured and found wanting, why then we have done no better than the men, have we. I see a kinder world for us."

From that moment on Rebecca was devoted to Florence and knew she would always be on her side against her brother, if there were a side to be on. She watched Zach critically throughout the day for any hint that he didn't know what a superior woman he had found. But he seemed to have sense enough to worship her. At dinnertime, the talk was about making a home out of the rudimentary house Zach had built on his land. Florence had many plans, and she and Philemon discussed bedding and curtains and plates. It seemed the women ruled the house that day.

There were two chuck wagons for the workers spaced far apart, and every week they were to move, following the men as the canal progressed. For now, Rebecca's stood under a lone cottonwood that would provide shade for a few hours in the heat of the day. The women's sleeping tent had been set up under the tree, and a tiny outhouse had gone into accommodating them.

"Now, ladies," Cookie said after he'd shown them their stores and equipment, "these men will be working long days in all weathers. Horse teams will be changed out through the day, but no one will change out the men. A man can work longer and harder on a full stomach, and your job is to see that he gets it." He pulled on a rope and the pantry box in the chuck wagon came down and turned into a worktable. Inside the wagon were two great Dutch ovens.

"You won't be putting the ovens away. You clean them out and start the next meal. Water barrel over here—the men will make sure you stay in wood and water. It's mush and bacon for breakfast, pork and beans and biscuits for lunch, stew and pancakes for supper."

Rebecca, LaRue, Minnie, and Lyla began with church hymns sung double time so the crew boss who supervised the men wouldn't think they were singing hymns. They laughed and chatted, but as the day wore on, the charm of outdoor cooking was tempered by exposure to sun and wind, the torment of flies, and the endless vast amounts of food required to feed the men.

They made a vat of molasses beans for lunch, and pan after pan of biscuits. It appeared that pork and beans appealed equally to flies as to men, and more than one greedy insect met its demise with a dive into the pot. Rebecca wouldn't eat the beans because of it.

They made a cauldron of beef stew and endless pancakes for supper, and by this time Rebecca was so hungry she ate the stew anyway, ignoring the possibility of unwelcome ingredients. The men came through the line tired and dusty and demanding. Cookie watched over to make sure they served the men up fine and glowered at the cooks if the men had any complaints about the food. She saw that LaRue bore up under it stoically, and even with good cheer. Rebecca tried to follow her example, but when one man, impatient, tried to grab the ladle from her, she smacked his hand. Luckily Cookie hadn't seen it, but LaRue did, and she tried to hide a smile.

That night Rebecca, in her clothes for she was too weary to undress, fell asleep to the sound of LaRue reading scriptures from the dear book. It seemed a little unfair of the dear book to ask her to Love the World when doing so seemed at times treacherous to her well-being. But next day, even though she was weary, she smiled at the first man in line and she smiled all the way through to the last man.

As days went by, she noted that the men had become friendlier with her, talking about the weather and such. Some one or two of the younger ones paid her little compliments as they went through the lines.

"Best spice at dinnertime is a lady's smile," said one, touching his hat.

"How does an angel come to be on a cook crew?" said another.

Some, of course, continued to be cranky. In her effort to Love the World, she was sure there must be a clause for forgiveness in the instance of particularly annoying persons.

If Coby came at the end of the line, when Rebecca was able to eat, she sat with him.

Once or twice a week, Radonna would come, clean and shiny and every hair in place, bearing a box of homemade cookies for the men. Often she would bring an extra little sack of cookies for Levi and sit with him while he ate them.

But one day Levi, coming through at the end of the line, asked Rebecca to sit with him. Rebecca took off her apron in a dream and floated behind him to the log where they would sit. She tucked her fingertips into her palms in case they weren't clean. She made small talk about the progress of the canal and how news had come that more settlers from Utah were making their way north to help with the work and earn some land. When Levi spoke, she tried to arrange her face artfully. She wondered if she were smiling too much, or not enough.

Then Levi said, "I heard you plan to buy land with your earnings, Rebecca."

How would he have known? One of her brothers must have told him.

"Yes, it's true."

"Well, I think it's a fine idea, no matter what others may say."

"You do?"

"I do," he said, and he looked into her eyes.

When you were young, she thought, you ran and played in a pack. One child was no different from another. You didn't notice yourself. No one minded you for good or bad. And then, one day, you picked one out to be special, and maybe he picked you back, and suddenly you felt like you were you for the first time . . .

"I mean to do it, now I've got this job," she said.

"I believe you. And I admire you." He stood. "Well, I'd best be getting back to work." He gave her his empty plate and was gone. She washed his plate very, very carefully.

Every Friday Cookie came to give them their wages,

and Rebecca rode home Saturday to put the money in her money box. Now it was beginning to fill up.

On one of her visits home, Florence and Zach were wed in the church, and Florence wore a classic black dress, which made her eyes look even more astonishingly blue. She and Zach moved into their house that afternoon.

When she was home, Rebecca watched Zach and Florence, holding hands, walking across the field to their little home, as if walking were the most delightful way to occupy one's time. She could see how they gave each other little special attentions, understood much in a word or two, knew when to tease and when to console, felt each other's little pains, and laughed when the other laughed, even when they hadn't heard the source of it. Gideon and Philemon had their own version of the same thing. Gideon's new family would be more to him than his old family now, for no one could fail to notice Philemon's growing belly. Rebecca surprised herself by feeling a bit lonely in a house with this much love going on. When Coby came over, as casually as if he were a son, and treated as much by Mother, it felt stiff and strange that they were the only ones not matched. But nobody else seemed to notice.

If there was time, Rebecca rode Tiny around Buffalo Flats, taking in the shadows in the grass, the doe that sprinted away, the frogs in the creek, the little life among the grasses, living and maybe not knowing they were living. She climbed the tor, took comfort in the slip of smoke coming from Coby's chimney, gazed at the valley, the prairie, the mountains beyond, and knew there was no more beautiful place in the world. Of course God had come here—he probably came often. Likely he'd been coming since the last day of creation, after he'd rested up some. It was a miracle, this land, and a miracle that her father and brothers had proved up this month and, so far, her family had made a go of living on it. She should be grateful enough for that. But you broke your heart over a rock like this. You did what you could to make it yours, that was all.

MAY DAY

M ay Day was considered the real first day of spring, and all the canal work would shut down for the holiday. There would be music and speeches in the churchyard, and then the march of the May Queen and King and their attendants in a floating line to the May Pole. They would weave the colored ribbons until the pole was pretty. After, there would be music and poetry and a picnic, and no matter what anyone else did, all eyes would be upon the May Queen.

The second Sunday of April, Brother Card announced who had been chosen. All the girls at church were modest about their chances, and especially LaRue. Girls who knew they had less chance—Jane who laughed in church at inappropriate times, Violet who was not old enough by a month, and Minnie who said she would hate for everyone to be looking at her—all of them were outspoken about who among the rest might be chosen queen and who might be princesses.

"Radonna is the prettiest, we all know that," said Violet. Radonna smiled.

"Rebecca is beautiful, too," LaRue said, and everyone looked at her. It was a dangerous thing to challenge Radonna's preeminence as the most beautiful, most deserving, most everything. For LaRue to do it was as astonishing as it was silencing.

"If you say such a thing again, LaRue, I will have to stop being your friend," Rebecca said, not meaning a word of it, of course.

LaRue looked pensive, or thoughtful, or maybe even sad. She seemed not to notice Radonna's dark look at her.

Rebecca said, "Whoever it is, we shall be glad and purge our hearts of envy so we needn't spend the first hundred years of eternity with green faces."

"Rebecca," Radonna said, "why do you say such outlandish things? There is no such doctrine."

The girls laughed, but LaRue stayed solemn and pale.

After church, Brother Card stood before the congregation as if it were the judgment bar itself. He congratulated everyone on the speedy progress of the canal, and assured them that more workers from the States were on their way, and he hoped they would be welcomed and helped as they settled into their new country. Then he said, "I know you have all been waiting to hear who will be the May Queen this year. I have discussed it with the members of the committee, and there was no doubt in anyone's mind that the most worthy young lady is ... LaRue Fletcher."

LaRue looked up, alarmed or confused—anything but happy.

Everyone in the room clapped.

"She was chosen for her good character and faithful ways. Her king shall be ..." He paused, and everyone laughed, for they all knew who it would be. "Ammon Leavitt, of course."

There was a good-natured cheer, but Ammon only smiled weakly.

Brother Card named the princesses: Radonna, Sympathy, and Rebecca.

And their corresponding princes: Coby, Ezra, and... Levi!

Rebecca almost clapped. Levi would be her escort. He came to her after the meeting.

"I'm glad it's me with you," he said.

"I'm glad, too," she said. Somehow it felt like fate that she had been paired with Levi. Maybe it was the world telling her something. Father said he didn't believe in fate, and neither did Coby. Did she? She looked up into Levi's face and decided she did.

Radonna seemed bitter, which offended Rebecca. She should be proud to have an escort like Coby. If she had a lick of sense, she would know that Coby was just as Mother said, the best boy God ever made out of dust.

Rebecca stopped herself, thinking that thought. Levi said something she didn't hear. She was looking for LaRue, but she was deep in conversation with Ammon, and they looked not to be disturbed.

The last Sunday of April, the May Day pole was erected and the long ribbons affixed for the practice. LaRue seemed somber and terribly queen-like while they all wove the ribbons around the pole—under, over, under, over—and unwound it and wound it again.

When the practice was over, bacon sandwiches and oatmeal cookies were handed out, and Rebecca left Levi to find LaRue collapsed on the grass. She said she wasn't hungry. She looked weary, a little sick, even, and LaRue was never weary or sick.

"What is it, LaRue? Are you not well?"

"Rebecca, I cannot do it. I am going to tell them it can't be me, it has to be you."

"But you've always thought it would be lovely to be May Queen! Tomorrow you will rise to the occasion, and you will make your parents and your brothers and Ammon and me proud."

LaRue grasped Rebecca's hand tightly with both of hers. "I cannot be May Queen, you see." She seemed to be pleading with Rebecca.

"You can and you must, LaRue. It makes me believe in a just world that you were chosen."

"Rebecca!" She shook Rebecca's hand. Her eyes were a washed-out blue, like the sky after a rain. "Please, I'm trying to tell you something..."

She began to rock herself a little, bowed over Rebecca's hand. "I am, I think—I am going to have a baby."

"Brother Card has decided and..."

"Rebecca!"

Rebecca felt herself catching up with herself, listening to, making sense of, the words she had already heard. They swirled around in her head, looking for a place to land, but there was no place in her mind where those words could sit down and make sense.

"You're going to...?"

LaRue made a sound like a newborn calf. "We only made one mistake…we promised we would be good from then on. I didn't think a baby could come of a moment."

Rebecca saw the world a painting then—a stretch of undefined prairie, a dust eddy spinning up and gone, a prairie mirage of water, a flock of unnamed birds. LaRue was the subject of the painting, her hair blowing, her ribbons, her skirt, her face looking away.

"You mustn't blame him, Rebecca, for it was me as much as him."

Him? Of course there was a him—there was always a him.

"Ammon." Rebecca flung his name into the air as if it were a great leggy insect that had landed on her.

"I love him, Rebecca. I will only be your friend if you will never speak against him. Do not test me on this."

LaRue had broken a commandment. LaRue and her brother, her own upright brother and her own perfect best friend. Why, she had thought LaRue so good! And now here she was, bad!

But that wasn't right.

Rebecca didn't know how, but she knew that was not right.

If she knew one thing, she knew there was something singularly and profoundly loving and good in her friend. If she knew one thing in the whole world it was that LaRue was good.

Rebecca's mind sorted. Everything she had thought was good and right seemed suddenly like phonics—a set of rules someone had made up but that didn't always apply.

LaRue with the light shining on her face, LaRue with the love in her eyes, LaRue who was surely beloved of the Lord—she was the beautiful word that broke the rules, just so you could see that it wasn't always the rules that were in charge of the world.

She stared into those eyes a long time, and her friend bore up under it. Maybe, Rebecca thought, maybe a broken commandment couldn't stay broken if it were touched by love. Maybe keeping a commandment locked away in a jewelry box so it could never be seen or touched—maybe that was a worse thing. Even a lie.

"Ammon knows?" Rebecca asked.

LaRue nodded. "Today he is fasting, and tonight he'll ask my father's permission to marry me."

Rebecca thought that might take more courage than Ammon had, for likely Brother Fletcher would strangle him with his bare hands. It would be well deserved, she thought, but that would leave LaRue without a father for her baby. Rebecca supposed she'd best hope Ammon survived—alive, but damaged enough to keep things in remembrance.

"And now you see why I cannot be May Queen," LaRue said.

Rebecca put her arms around her friend and held her until her shoulders ceased to shake.

"Ammon will tell them why," LaRue said. "So there can be no discussion."

"You don't need to tell them why. You don't need to tell them anything."

"People will know. Someday."

"They'd best not judge," Rebecca said. "They'd best not disappoint me. It's hard enough to Love the World."

"Rebecca, Ammon and I, though we never said it...we had high hearts because of the praise of others. Now will we say it's unfair if they speak against us? If one, then the other. You must take my place on May Day."

"No."

"No?"

"You are still the best soul on earth. Of course you must be May Queen. Don't you want to make me happy?"

"Rebecca, how can I before God?"

"Because if anyone deserved to be crowned with flowers on a spring day and set above others for a few moments, it is you, LaRue. I don't care if they mind."

"God might mind."

"God will mind the least."

"Don't speak of him as if you'd met him personally. Tomorrow I will be a married woman, and you will be May Queen."

If Mother had not stood before her son to protect him, Brother Fletcher would not have had any opportunity to strangle Ammon, for Ammon's own father would have had all the pleasure. As it was, Father took his leave to the Vicary field and stayed there a long time. He came back smelling of tobacco and looking as if the fight had gone out of him. Ammon was harnessing the team for the journey to the Fletcher house, and Rebecca helped.

"I will come with you," Father said to Ammon.

Ammon said nothing.

"It is my shame, too. I will tell him that you and yours will be provided for until your house is furnished and you are on your feet."

"I'm coming, too," Rebecca said. "LaRue will need me."

No one said anything to the contrary.

LaRue and her father came to the door together, LaRue just behind her father. Brother Fletcher didn't look at Father, and so Rebecca knew that he had been apprised of things.

"Sir, Brother Fletcher, sir," Ammon began. "Please. I—I know I'm unworthy even to be here and ask forgiveness. But I believe—I know that out of this will come great good, for I love and honor your daughter and I beg your permission to marry her. You know I've wanted to marry her for a long time."

"You will go now, Ammon," Brother Fletcher said after a long silence. His voice was calm and low.

"Sir, please tell me what I can do—"

"Don't 'please sir' me one more time, young man, as if to show respect. You have shown me in deed how much respect you have for me, by the way you dishonored my daughter." He looked at Father at last. "Samuel, I do not blame you, but you must know that this will affect our dealings, for which I am sorry. Goodbye."

"Brother Fletcher, please," Ammon said. "I love her. I want to marry her. I will take care of her, I promise!"

"You aren't good enough for her. Even in her condition, you aren't good enough for her. Everyone doted on her, admired her, and yet she wanted to be your girl...Now you have taken her down."

LaRue was weeping behind her father. "Father, no—"

"Please tell me what to do. I'll do anything," Ammon pleaded, and Rebecca could see that there were tears in his eyes.

"It's not for you to cry," Brother Fletcher said. "It's for LaRue to cry and for you to be a man if you ever can. She'll be confined to home now, and when she has the baby, she will give it to my childless sister in Idaho."

"But—but the baby—it's mine, too!"

"Last I checked, young man, her last name was my last name, not yours. You are confused. Now you get on, and pray my daughter one day finds someone who's good enough for her, if any such man will have her."

"Please, for the love of God..."

"Don't speak to me about the love of God. It's by the love of God that I let you walk this earth."

The door slammed.

They were silent most of the way home.

Finally, Father said, "Well, that went as well as could be expected."

Rebecca and Ammon looked at him and then at each other.

"It's what I would have said, had it been my daughter," Father said. "He'll think about things, now that he's got that off his chest. And his wife and daughter and his own good nature will work on him. He'll come around."

"Do you think so, Father?" Ammon said.

"Of course he will," Rebecca said. "Shame for asking— of course he will."

She reached over and took Ammon's hand, and he squeezed it back mightily.

Rebecca wore, as May Queen, a white gown with lace at the collar, sleeves, and hem, passed down from the May Queen the year before and the year before that. Her hair flowing past her hips was allowed to curl as much as it liked. The escorts, through some machinations of Radonna, likely, had been changed. Coby would be Rebecca's escort, and Levi, Radonna's.

When Coby saw her, his Adam's apple went up and down as if it would disgorge that fateful bite.

"You look beautiful," he said.

"So do you," she said, and she suddenly found she didn't mind about the switch. She put her land lightly on his arm, and the procession began.

She walked with her head high, her heart low. The attendants, with their partners in hand, followed behind, until they came to the May Pole and began the ribbon dance to the music of the fiddle and the applause of the congregation.

Rebecca danced round the May Pole with her ribbon, and she thought of her LaRue and that all goodness and badness was just such a ribbon thing: under and over, round and round, under, over, until it seemed all the good and bad in the world couldn't be told one from the other. They wove the pole, and unwove it, and wove it again, under, over, round, and round, to the music, the sweet music, the white and the blue and the red ribbons, and her hair was down and Coby looking as if something inside him had relented. The congregation applauded again when they were done, and everything was as it had always been and as it always would be, and yet nothing was the same.

PHILEMON'S BABY

The relentless and tedious work of cooking for the men on the canal held few compensations for Rebecca without LaRue to talk and laugh with. Only the thought of her black enameled box and what was inside gave her some comfort.

She had been adding it up in her head all along, but she had never counted it, not once. What if she were off? What if she counted and she wasn't even close? She couldn't bear it if she wasn't close. Better not to know. But now after working for months it was time to know.

The next Saturday she was home, she got out her money box.

She counted once, twice, three times.

The first time, it added up to four hundred ninety-four dollars.

The second time, it added up to four hundred ninety-four dollars.

The third time, it added up to four hundred ninety-four dollars.

She had enough for her land.

Since May, Mother had given Rebecca time on Sundays to visit LaRue and bring a loaf of fresh bread or a pie or a basket of eggs. Rebecca was never invited in, but as she stood at the door,

Sister Fletcher would tactfully become occupied with baby Abigail and leave Rebecca and LaRue alone for a few minutes. Rebecca would pass LaRue a letter from Ammon, and LaRue would pass one back. Ammon, when he received it, would go off to the barn to read it alone. Once, with tears, Ammon secretly told Rebecca that he would run away with LaRue when the baby was born. Rebecca said she saw Brother Fletcher greet Father civilly at church once, and maybe he wouldn't have to steal her away, but Ammon shook his head hopelessly.

This visit, after they embraced and exchanged notes, Rebecca handed over some preserves, and said, "LaRue, I have enough to buy my land."

"Rebecca, that's wonderful!"

"I'm going to stop working on the canal," she said.

But before LaRue could respond, her mother was back, and it was time to go.

Rebecca returned home to find Philemon standing in the doorway, cradling her belly.

"Are you all right, Philemon? Where's Mother?"

"She went to visit Sister Gladden. Oh, Rebecca, I think it's time."

No, Rebecca thought, it isn't time. It's surely too early... "Come," Rebecca said, and she led her to bed. "I'll ride out to the herd and get Gideon. It's probably nothing."

"Don't leave me, please. Rebecca... Is this right? It's too early! Is it supposed to hurt so and never stop?"

"It will be fine. Everything will be fine. Mother will be here soon, and first babies take a long time, I'm sorry to say. Also don't forget, I've delivered a baby or two before."

"The blessing, please, Rebecca," Philemon said.

Rebecca put her hands on Philemon's head. "Philemon Leavitt, angel and beloved sister of Rebecca Leavitt, you have blessed our whole family by marrying Gideon, and you will undoubtedly go to heaven for it. And now have your baby. Amen."

It wasn't long after the blessing that Gideon came home, having gone to his own house to check on his wife and finding her gone.

And it wasn't long after that the baby was born.

Mother still had not yet arrived, but the baby was born perfectly formed and beautiful, though small.

"It's a boy," Rebecca said, pleased with herself as if the baby were her own.

"It's a boy!" Gideon said.

"It's a boy," Philemon said. She held out her arms, but Rebecca didn't give her the baby.

The baby did not struggle for air, though his eyes were open just a little.

She scooped out his mouth. He was a dusky color, gray as glacier ice.

He would cry soon.

She cut the umbilical cord. He would cry any moment.

She flicked his heel as she had seen Mother do. She wrapped him in a warm towel. Rubbed him.

"Come on," Rebecca said. She pushed gently at his tiny chest. "Come on...You must fight for it, little one," she said. A bit of sunlight was trembling in the room, just at the side of her vision.

"I can't hear him," Philemon said.

"Breathe," Rebecca said like a prayer.

"Is he okay?" Gideon asked.

"Breathe," Rebecca said. "You must try—"

But his whole body was still... What was that light, that shimmering column of light in her eyes?

"Come now," Rebecca said, and her whole body was a prayer. She wondered if she had ever prayed before, now that she was praying with her whole body and on her feet, standing on her feet.

She remembered Elijah, and how in the scripture story he put his mouth onto the mouth of the dead boy. Rebecca put her mouth on the baby's tiny mouth and breathed. She breathed from the roots of her lungs, but he would not breathe back—

Philemon cried, "Why isn't he crying?"

Gideon left his wife's side and took the baby in his arms, but he was helpless. All those muscles in his shoulders and chest, but that baby could not be muscled into breathing.

Mother opened the door, and the thread of light, thin and lithe as a boy, slipped out as she came in.

Gideon, holding his baby, cried out for Mother.

Rebecca ran.

She could see him, a slender, heatless core of light, escaping over the grass tops, fleet as a hawk's shadow. Now she thought she could see him as a boy, long-limbed, long-haired, light. She could never run as fast as him.

She mounted Tiny and rode after him, westward toward the mountains. She knew where he was going.

She rode Tiny hard to the tor, dismounted before he'd fully stopped, and ran up the tor. Hadn't the little one led her this way? Hadn't he given her teasing glimpses of him, a bright shadow, a glossy bit of wind, a white bird flitting away?

The Sitting Rock looked smaller, softer, dustier, as if she'd been away a thousand years, as if it had been frozen a thousand times since she'd seen it last and the slightest touch would shatter it.

She walked around the rock, staring out over the flats, looking for the baby, the boy, but light was everywhere. Too many places to hide. He had been here, but he could be at the mountains by now — past the lower fortress of trees, higher than the ice melt snaking down the mountain, perhaps as high as the pale bare rock where the clouds steamed. She stood and stared out over the flats for however long it was and could not think a thing.

She heard a footstep.

It was Coby.

She turned and faced him.

"I was at your house. I told your mother I knew where to find you," he said.

The moon was pale and thin in the day sky, weightless as a dandelion seed.

"Your mother said — she said to say that with this kind, there is nothing to be done. That you mustn't blame yourself."

Nothing to be done? Why? He had been so perfect...

"Philemon is asking for you," Coby said.

She considered that.

"He came this way," she said. Her voice was old-sounding, a grandmother's voice. "The baby. I saw him. Like a spindle of light — he ran like a coyote —"

She wanted to tell Coby why she knew the boy would come here. She wanted to tell him why this wasn't just any old rock. She wanted to tell him that only now did she realize she had blessed Philemon, selfishly, with not a word about the baby. And now the baby had got away. Of course he would want to get away, of course. Why would he want to come to a world where it hurt to breathe and to love, where any day your heart could be halved without warning...?

Coby came to her side, and they looked across the flats to the mountains.

"Philemon would have been a good mother," she said.

"She would have," he said. "She still will be, someday."

"Only she would have made him read Isaiah," Rebecca said.

"And learn his multiplication tables," he said.

"And clean out the chicken coop," she said.

He put his hand on her back, gently, to lead her down the tor. She turned and put her head on his chest and began to cry. She cried for Philemon and Gideon and for the empty Sitting Rock. She cried for Ammon and LaRue, longing for each other and not allowed to see each other. She cried because she was crying.

He put his arms around her.

"You only get to cry once when you're a grown-up," she said, straightening and stepping away.

Coby nodded.

"Then you stop and get on with it," she said.

She got on with it.

When she got home, Gideon met her at the door, took her hand, and gently—how could such a big man be so gentle?—guided her to Philemon. Philemon embraced her, but this time she had no words. Nothing was said. Nothing could be said.

Later Mother came to her room to brush Rebecca's hair. She was always gentle, but this night she was gentler than ever.

"Mother, I wonder, please, would you teach me the art of midwifing? I'd like to learn nursing, too. I'd like to learn everything you know. I mean, really learn."

"Of course, Rebecca."

"And Mother, I think I'll give notice to the cook boss. That way I can come with you whenever you're called."

"But Rebecca, the money for your land . . ."

"I have it now. I have enough. And you know, Mother, with all the new folks coming, it's like enough someone will need my job. And they'll all need nurses and midwives."

"Yes. I will teach you."

Mother looked at her with pride. She was truly proud, Rebecca could tell. And now she realized this was not the first time she'd seen that look. Rebecca realized she'd seen it often. She realized, then, that she'd been raised on it.

The church sisters brought food—the family wouldn't have to cook for a week—and Radonna brought three of her famous rhubarb pies. Rebecca said thank you, and watched Radonna ride away until she couldn't see her anymore. What was it about pie that meant so much at a sad time? Rebecca didn't know, but Radonna knew.

Philemon wanted no funeral, only prayer and a few tears at the grave site. One of Gideon's boots couldn't have fit into the little casket. Inside, wrapped in a receiving blanket his mother had made for him, the baby, skin like candle wax. Gideon and Philemon carried their sorrow in their arms like an infant. One day they would have to lay it down, but for now they carried it everywhere. Philemon's bodice was always wet, soaked with milk. Her breasts hadn't given up on that baby.

After the little casket had joined its fellows in the cemetery and the family had gone home, Rebecca stayed in the cemetery alone. She dismounted and stood in the wind and the quiet. For now, it was a little cemetery with only a few headstones. And now there was one for Kincaid, the name Gideon and Philemon had given their infant son. People buried their loved ones far apart, leaving room for the rest of the family, for those who were to come, as if they were staking their claim for a family picnic there on resurrection morning.

She was appalled by the little headstone and the grief it represented, the arms of the mother bereft, clutching at nothing, not knowing right-side up or down, flailing for something to hold. Some might wonder that such a mother could bend her knees to pray, but such knees would have no strength — such were feeble knees, and once down, they were down.

Mother had once said the sorrow of a baby's tombstone was tempered by the assurance that little children went straight to heaven and no one need worry about the state of their souls in the eternities. But Mother hadn't said it to Gideon or Philemon. It would be no comfort to them, not yet, not for a long time, and maybe never. Rebecca wondered if Kincaid would be a bit resentful, upon entering the gates of heaven, saying, it was brief, Lord.

She stood and walked among the tombstones and then returned to sit down next to her baby nephew. The ground under her felt restful, as if it were her ancient grandfather letting her sit on his lap.

Kincaid Leavitt, the tombstone said, and the year of death. That was all. He had come to get a tombstone out of life, and to cause exquisite grief. She thought that the dust beneath her was whispering something she didn't want to hear.

If she saw God again, she would tell him all this. He would likely know, but he wouldn't mind her telling him anyway. He was like that. She would tell and tell and tell, until she was done telling. That, she suspected, was part of what eternity was for.

FLOOD

The canal work carried on in the heat and the rain and the wind.

Rebecca stayed home with Mother now, but Ammon worked until he felt he was digging down to hell. He didn't complain, in keeping with Father's lost eleventh commandment. The first furrow had tempted Rebecca to plant potatoes in it, but now she saw that it was going to be deep and straight and would water a land.

She had been surprised when she learned that all rivers ran to the sea. She had thought the rivers would run out of the sea to water the land, the sea having so much to share. But no, water was always seeking the sea. Water was an escaping thing—crashing down mountains in foaming cataracts to creeks and streams and rushing rivers, all running to the sea, to the sea! But now people were going to divert some of it, and the water in the canals would forget the sea and soak into the dry soil. Now more people would come and would stay and would grow grain to feed nations, and drink the water that had forgotten the sea, might never get to the sea, not in a thousand thousand years...

But she had her money, and the very first day Coby could get away, he and she and Father would go to the land office. Coby would relinquish his preemption rights, and on the spot, Rebecca and Father would buy the land. Her name would be on the deed. Father's, too, but only as a formality. It would be her land at last.

It snowed. In August. It melted two days later, except in the mountains where there was a heavy snow. Father said he'd never heard of such a place for weather.

The weather turned warm again, and then it rained. For three days it rained until Mother almost complained by saying she could hardly breathe in such wet air. And then one night, just before dawn, it stopped. It was so strange, that dry silence, that Rebecca woke up. Mother was up, too. Rebecca helped Mother make breakfast and after Father left to find Gideon and Zach so they could check on the cattle. She went out to the barn with the milk pails, daydreaming of the look on the land agent's face when she walked into his office and put her money on that counter. She imagined Queen Victoria smiling down at her from her place on the wall. So deep in her thoughts was she that she almost didn't notice the river.

She almost didn't notice that something was wrong.

What?

What was different?

A sound.

A strange sound.

Or — not really a sound, but a terrible silence. It took her a moment to realize that the river was no longer rushing by. It had lowered suddenly, as if for the Israelites to cross the Jordan. Then it did make a sound — a sick sound, or an angry sound, she couldn't tell. The water had gone dark.

Rebecca ran to the house. "Mother, the river is — the river is holding its breath!"

Mother had her back to her. Her spine stiffened, and her neck seemed to stretch. Slowly she turned and said in a low voice, "Run up the rise, Rebecca, to the barn."

Such a strange thing to say in so calm a voice. Rebecca stared at her. Her mother's lips were gray. "Run up the rise," she said again. "To the top. I'll be right behind you."

Something in Mother's voice made Rebecca stare.

"Rebecca, run!" Mother shouted, and Rebecca noted that it was the first time she had ever heard her mother shout at her.

Rebecca ran.

She ran as fast as she could up the rise.

Once at the top she saw Mother only then leaving the house. She was running wildly, her apron clutched to her chest as if it were a child.

Rebecca started to go to help her, but Mother waved at her furiously and shouted at her to stay.

Rebecca knew she was afraid.

Mother was never afraid.

Upriver she saw mud-brown water shouldering through the riverbed like a gigantic grizzly. It was all paws and claws, pushing, hunched, and roaring as if it pursued something. The thick waters surged around their house, the grizzly flood opened its mouth.

Mother arrived at the top in time to watch with Rebecca as the house tipped over, toppled full on its side, and floated away. Tumbling down the river behind were their beds and tables and chairs and quilts and cups and the pictures of Joseph and Hyrum, and the queen.

She and Mother could not speak.

Mother stood clutching that ridiculous apron to her

chest, staring down at the place where their house had been. Even the river was silent now, muddy and brown and fast, but lowering.

The silence was trying to tell Rebecca something, something she didn't want to know.

"Oh, Mother," she said, "oh Mama, my money box..."

Mother had to pull her gaze away from the river. She fumbled with her apron, and produced out of its folds Rebecca's black enameled money box.

Rebecca stared at it. It was more terrifying to think that Mother had risked her life to rescue it than it had been to think it had been lost.

Mother held it out to her, but Rebecca didn't know if she had the strength at that moment to carry such a weighty thing. She held Mother instead.

When Father found them, he leaned his head on his wife's neck and wept. "Thank the Lord," he said over and over. Which Rebecca thought was rather generous of him, given that the Lord had just swept away his house and it was likely floating toward the sea at this very moment. Coby came galloping and was off his horse before it had fully stopped. He said nothing, just stared at the mud where the house used to be, walked in little circles, and stared again.

Gideon and Zach had gone to check on Philemon and Florence, and they all soon joined them. Only then did Rebecca consider how close she and Mother had come to sailing down the river alongside their beds and belongings.

They watched the river for a long time. It had gone down some, but it hadn't given up on trying to wash the world away. A tree floated by, a chicken coop with a chicken perched on the top, a drowned cow, a boot...

Father finally said, "Let's go to Gideon's place."

Her brothers' properties had new ponds on them, but not being close to the river they had otherwise been spared. Some people up- and downriver had also suffered losses, and Ammon, who had ridden home from the canal, reported that part of it had been taken out. Only her family had lost their entire house. The potato field and Mother's garden were fine. Last year's leftovers of flour and rice and oats were gone, but thankfully they hadn't purchased the winter's supply yet. Lost were Mother's precious bottled peas and beans and berries, but Father said with forced cheer that he never liked peas anyway.

People who had not been flooded out came to commiserate. But though her people preached the gospel of love for one's fellow man, and service to others, somehow, Rebecca noted, Father felt it a shame to accept help from one's neighbor. Rebecca thought it a perplexing arithmetic problem: take the number of people who are supposed to serve one another, which was everyone, and subtract the number of people who will not be served if they can help it, and you have...

But her church family were not troubled by arithmetic. Women brought pots and pots of food. It was all her brothers could do to eat it all. A member of her church might die of despair, but they would do it on a full stomach.

Levi brought Father a beautiful horse. Just brought it. A whole horse.

"It's just a horse, with a leg on each corner," he said, as if it were nothing.

"I'm not short a single horse because of the flood, I'm grateful to say," Father said, declining the gift.

But Levi said his land couldn't support another horse, and it would be doing him a kindness if Father would take it off his hands. He rode off before Father could protest.

Gideon and Philemon seemed as delighted as they were allowed to be, given the disaster that had happened, to have them all in their home, but it was a home that had been built for two and perhaps two little ones. After a sleep and many prayers of thanks, the family went back to where their house had been. They found a few of Mother's pewter utensils, one iron cooking pot hanging from a bush, and a bullet mold. Farther down the river, they found Mother's cookstove, lying feet-up on the bank. Even the tempest couldn't bully that beast to the sea.

The cattle had been nowhere near the river. But to sell enough stock to replace the house and every possession they owned would deplete the herd and make it impossible to carry on. Even with all the extras their church family brought — clothes, cooking utensils, quilts — there wasn't enough.

"Children," Father said, "we have much to be thankful for, given that your mother and sister came out of this alive. It goes without saying that this is the most important thing. But your mother and I have talked, and we feel the only answer is to go back to Utah — your mother and I and Rebecca. I'll find work in the mines and save for a new house. If we return, we hope we come back to find the land cared for as your own, between the three of you. And if we don't come back, well, the land would have been yours anyway."

Rebecca made a sound. She herself didn't know what that sound meant. Her mouth seemed to know it had something to say before the rest of her did.

"I wish people would consult me before they decide what is to be and what isn't."

They all looked at her wearily, as if to say that now was not the time to exhibit her peculiarities of character. She fetched her money box. Everyone stared at her hands shaking as she opened it.

"In here is the money I've been saving for my—for the land. You must take it, Father, and begin again. If you need more, you can sell that horse Levi brought, my cow and pig, and if Ammon contributes a little from his work on the canal, you can build a new house and purchase what you need to stay and get through the winter."

"Oh, Rebecca," Mother said.

Father stared at the money. He said, his voice unsteady, "But how can I take it? A grown man, from his own daughter?"

"I know you are a man of great pride," Rebecca said, "but you must accept it. You must consider the feelings of your wife and daughter who have no wish to leave. If you are concerned that I will lord it over you—well, I admit I will probably be tempted at times. But it would be a small price to pay, would it not, Father?"

Mother bowed her head and folded her hands before her mouth.

"But you must promise we shall never leave," Rebecca said, holding out the box.

Father took up the box and held it in his two hands.

After a long moment, he said, "I promise." And he took Rebecca in his arms.

The river could take their house and all the little mankind comforts inside it—chairs and stools, pots and spoons, needles and buttons and beds—but it hadn't taken their land. They would build a new house, on higher ground.

Work had resumed on the canal, but it was decided that Ammon wouldn't return so he could help build the house and get ready for winter.

The next day Rebecca rode to the tor and sat a long time.

She sat under the gaze of the great-uncle mountains, their usual disapproval tinged by some sort of familial sympathy. She hoped these mountains wouldn't be ashamed of being loved by her.

It was her saddest day.

On her saddest day, why wouldn't he be here?

It made you wonder why then and not now.

It made you feel longing and lonesome.

It was to be a two-story lumber house.

"Spruce beetles come out of the logs," she said. "I hate to think of them crawling over me at night." And so it was decided. Rebecca, she found, now more often got her way.

Father and Mother lived with Gideon and Philemon, and Rebecca stayed with Zach and Florence. Evenings on the porch, while they sewed, she and Florence would air their grievances about suffrage. Zach would listen and sometimes nod. But the next day Florence would serve

Zach as if he were a lord, and she seemed to find no contradiction in this.

Many hands came to help build the house, which they built in a safer location, including LaRue's father, who wielded a hammer as if the nails were Ammon's head. Few words were spoken between the respective fathers, but something softened. That was what happened when you lived your religion, Rebecca supposed, and she also supposed she'd never forget it. Coby was there every day when his own work was done. Levi came often, too, and the two of them seemed to try and outdo each other in their efforts to help. Levi praised Rebecca for paying for the house. She had asked her family not to tell others where they got the money, but somehow it had got out. Coby said she had only done what family did. Other men from church came to help, too, and even a few of the Cochrane cowboys came out. The only one who never came was Brother Sempel.

Rebecca couldn't be sad to hear that the flood had taken out part of the canal, because with it went the vision of this place dotted with great cities, at least for a little while. Land investors back east tore their hair out: Is it flood or famine? No one could predict. She was glad the land was so hard to tame, with blizzards sometimes in June, and shirtsleeve weather sometimes in December, and Chinooks any time of year. She was glad it was a land of unshaded heat in summer, horseflies as big as sparrows, and drought and thunderstorms and hail. Sometimes, she guessed, he who loved Sunsets wanted his rivers to flood up like a Revenge and the glaciers to pour endlessly down the sides of his mountains like a Testimony.

THE BARN

By the end of September the house was dried in, Mother's kitchen was complete, and they'd built some furniture, so they moved in. The house would have a real parlor, once winter set in and the men had more time for the indoor finishing work. Rebecca insisted that come spring Mother would have a stuffed sofa for her parlor, shipped all the way from Calgary, and Mother said nobody would be allowed to sit on it except on Sundays.

They had enough money left over to restock the cellar with flour, oats, rice, dried beans, and to buy a few other essentials necessary for their day-to-day lives—plates, glasses, silverware, and jars to use to preserve for winter what was still left in Mother's garden, given what a late start they were getting. Philemon and Florence gave them their extra sewing and embroidery tools and knitting needles. They had slaughtered a pig and later in the fall, the men would hunt for deer so they could put up some venison. There would be no Christie Brown and Company First Prize Golden Graham Wafers this year, but even so, they would be as ready for winter as they could be.

One morning shortly after they had settled into the new house, Rebecca went to do the milking and found an old friend, Sempel's milch cow, in their barn again. Just be good, Father had said, so she sighed and led it out of the barn with a handful of alfalfa. This time, however, there were no other cows in sight to tempt her away. She settled on putting a rope around the cow's neck, saddling Tiny, and making her way to the Sempels'.

The Sempel homestead always had a bare, lonely feeling to it. There were no children running about. The yard needed picking up, and no flowers had been planted. The chickens roosted silently in a nearby tree, and the hog slept.

As she approached the door, she thought she heard weeping coming from inside. She knocked, and the weeping immediately stopped.

Rebecca waited, but no one came to the door. She called, "Hello? Sister Sempel? I brought your milch cow, which was eating our hay again."

After a long moment she heard someone stirring.

"Thank you, Rebecca," Sister Sempel said through the door. "I apologize for our cow."

"Sister Sempel, are you well?"

There was a short silence.

"I'm well enough. Good day, Rebecca," she said.

Rebecca put her hand on the door latch, though why, she couldn't have said, and pulled. There stood Sister Sempel, her dress torn, and bruises on her face and throat. She held her arm as if it had been injured.

Rebecca took a step back and stared at the woman. "I'll bring Mother," she said quietly.

"No. Rebecca, no. Please go home. It—It isn't safe

here." She moved her hand in warning, and winced. "He'll be back soon."

"I will take you to Mother, then," Rebecca said.

"He'll look for me there and it will be the worse for me. Please, Rebecca, go."

Rebecca jumped on Tiny and made him run all the way home.

Mother listened to her without a word and retired to her room for a time. When she came out, she sent Rebecca to her sisters-in-law's homes to invite them to supper. That afternoon Mother baked a ham and made scalloped potatoes, dinner rolls, and delicious vinegar pie. Rebecca helped her prepare the food and did not ask what ham had to do with helping Sister Sempel, for Mother still hadn't said a word to her about it.

After everyone had arrived, Ammon asked, "What feast is this?" looking at the ham glistening in a glaze of brown sugar.

"It is an Esther feast," Mother said, "a meal to soften the heart."

"Well, my heart is soft as summer butter just looking at it," Father said.

Mother prayed the blessing, which was full of gratitude for her husband who exercised his authority with persuasion, long-suffering, gentleness and meekness and love unfeigned. Father was blushing by the time his wife said amen.

Gideon carved the ham and Father passed him his plate. Mother put nothing on her plate, and Florence and

Philemon very little. The men began to serve themselves creamy potatoes when Father noticed that Mother wasn't talking or passing.

"Are you well, Liza?" he asked.

She cleared her throat. "Today, Samuel, Rebecca took the Sempel cow home."

"Ah. Neighborly of you, Rebecca," Father said.

He picked up his fork and knife, though his eyes were fixed on his wife's face.

"You will be horrified to know what she saw there," Mother said in her most genteel voice. "Rebecca?"

"Her arm was injured, and she had bruises on her face and neck..." Rebecca didn't recognize her own voice.

Father's knife and fork were poised in the air above his plate. He looked at his wife, at Rebecca, at his sons, their wives, and back again at his wife. Rebecca saw that each of her brothers was concentrating on his own meal as if a gold coin was hidden in it.

"You and I have long suspected what has been going on there," Mother said in a voice that was like a mild breeze on a glacier field. "And now we have proof. It is time that he — that man — was held to account by someone his own size."

Rebecca had never seen this woman before, so cool, so straight of back and high of chin, so powerfully armed by her previous decades of devotion to her husband and family, speaking the unspeakable at the dinner table before them all.

Mother's gaze swung in dignified containment from her husband to her sons and back again, the way a heavy church door swings solemnly on its hinges.

Father cleared his throat and everyone waited for him to speak.

"There's a reckoning to be made by every man who mistreats or, God forbid, strikes a woman," he said. "Treat a woman like she's the best thing God ever made, and you'll be right every time and never be sorry. I hate to think I would have to say such a thing, that I should have to be so blunt, but now it is said, in case there was any doubt of it."

There was a silence, and Father started eating, having put the world to rights again.

"And what will you do, then, about Pietr Sempel, husband?" Mother asked.

Father let his cutlery fall to the plate with clear exasperation. Rebecca had never seen Father do something so dismissive.

Ammon said, "Excuse me from the table, please."

"No," Mother said, "you are not excused."

Of course, Leavitts were never afraid—Rebecca knew they did not give way or give in or give up. But right now they were all a little afraid. They were afraid of Mother.

Her brothers looked down at their plates, apparently not presuming upon their right to seconds. Nor did any of them seem to wish to distinguish themselves any more by requesting to leave the table. They sat hunched and hoping to be forgotten. Mother looked on her husband and sons as if she were considering the method of their execution.

"Tomorrow," Mother said, "you, Samuel, and my big, strong sons, will pay a visit to Brother Sempel."

Mother put a teaspoon of peas on her plate, daintily,

as if the problem would go away now. Father looked with foreboding at Mother's teaspoon of peas.

"We should discuss this between ourselves, Liza," Father said tersely. Rebecca had never seen Father be terse with Mother before.

"We will discuss it before our sons and our daughter and our daughters-in-law, so they might know what is right and what is wrong. Samuel, you must take Sister Sempel away and send her someplace she can be safe."

"My dear, we shall not be part of separating a husband and a wife. Does not the scripture say, 'Let not the wife depart from her husband,'" Father said. "Only for adultery are we excused to be put apart, and I doubt he has committed adultery."

Rebecca thought, because no one would have him.

"And what commandment," said Mother, "is more serious than 'thou shalt not commit adultery'? 'Thou shalt not kill.' And he's like to kill that woman one of these days—if she doesn't die of a broken heart first. Will you stand by until it is too late, Samuel?"

Father, at the head of the table, stood up suddenly. The chair, pushed back by his rising, made an angry sound.

Mother, at the end of the table, also stood up, elegantly, her chair making not a sound.

"Liza, we won't discuss it any further. It is none of our business," Father said.

"And this is what you have to say to me?" Mother said quietly to her husband.

"This is what I have to say to you," Father replied.

Mother looked at him for a long moment in silence. And

then, without doing the dishes first, Mother moved her rocking chair and herself into the barn.

Rebecca's brothers were willing enough to help make Mother comfortable in the barn, until they heard that Florence and Philemon would also be joining her.

Rebecca would have to keep the house running, Mother said evenly. Gideon and Zach slept in the parental house that night instead of their own homes, as if their homes didn't interest them without their wives in them. The next morning they were up at the usual time, but they moped about as if there'd been a death in the family.

Rebecca must cook. She knew how to assemble ingredients — she just didn't know how to tame the dragon that was Mother's cookstove. Its encounter with the flood hadn't made it any less temperamental. Only Mother knew when it was just hot enough, which she judged by holding her hand over it. So the breakfast porridge was lumpy and the scrambled eggs dry and crispy. Still the men ate, though glumly. No sooner had she cleaned up than it was time to work on lunch. She made beans and biscuits for lunch, having had much practice with them, but the beans were crunchy, and the biscuits a bit burnt on the bottom. She served it shamefaced to her mother and sisters in the barn, and all Mother would say was that food always tasted better when it was cooked by someone else. Rebecca had no time to feel sorry for herself, for she must do all her own chores and Mother's also.

As one day and then another wore on, Rebecca began to understand how a woman became essential to a man with no greater credit to her name than that she bent herself daily over her stove, her garden, and in consecrating her time and talents to the nurturing of her children. This labor, this endless labor, was enough to defeat someone who up until now had only had to help. She thought about starting on the bottling but she couldn't imagine how she would manage.

Father's face seemed to have aged overnight. At the end of the second day he came home early and looked out the window toward the barn a long time. He ate the beans and biscuits Rebecca had cooked again. That evening he went out to the barn. What they may have said to each other while he was there, Rebecca didn't know. If it had anything to do with trying to lure his wife back into the house, it didn't work.

He went to bed without calling for family prayer. Rebecca couldn't remember a time when she'd gone to bed without family prayer.

The next day after breakfast, Rebecca went down to the barn to do the milking and to seek solace.

The barn was filled with the heavy and sharp things of men, the chains and leathers that bound the horses to their whims, the shovels and spikes and plough blades and saws—everything meant to tame or conquer. And among all that, in a stall, the floor of it covered in fresh hay, was her mother—soft and clean and unconquerable—and her sisters-in-law at Mother's feet like ladies-in-waiting.

Rebecca did her best to persuade her mother to come home.

"Father doesn't know what to do with himself," Rebecca said.

"We have given him a bit of a shock is all. Give him time to think things through."

"He's not even angry. It's awful."

Mother stroked her hair. "Rebecca. Sometimes — sometimes a body must stand for something, and sometimes, when we do, we will offend."

"You never offend. You are an angel, at least you were until now."

"Some people think I am an angel because I do not express contradictory opinions, and they think it is because I cannot. They think I am a shadow and that they can walk right through me. But they misunderstand angels, and they are going to bump into me now. They will see that I will not move to the right or the left, and they are going to have to trouble themselves to walk around me."

"You are brave, Mother."

"Rebecca, you mustn't admire me. I drew a line, and now your father or I must cross over it. If he loses, I lose, too."

"But if you win, he wins, too."

"Let us hope he is able to see it that way. For now, you must take care of your father and brothers as best you can."

Thinking she would try something different for supper, she had Father kill one of their chickens. She thought she remembered from her box lunch how to prepare it, but when she served it up it was as dry as dirt.

Her brothers were gentle with her and said nothing about the food, as if their trial had made them rise above personal resentments, as if, now that they had become martyrs, they must suffer in silence. Her brothers probably hoped Father would surrender before they starved to death.

She hadn't had time to weed the potato field, so the weeds went to sleep that night wondering how they had managed to live another day. She went to her bed exhausted.

In the morning, Rebecca and the cookstove seemed to come to some kind of understanding. The pancakes were fluffy and the eggs were done just right. The bacon was crisping up nicely.

Father would be relieved, she thought. It wouldn't be so bad for Mother to be in the barn, if only he could get a decent meal —

She stopped. She studied the perfect pancakes and eggs.

And then she put them back in their respective pans.

When Father sat down for his breakfast, he found burned pancakes, charred bacon, and crispy eggs.

Father took himself to the barn.

Rebecca followed not far behind with the milking pails.

When Father came before Mother and her daughters-in-law, holding his hat in his two hands, Mother looked up and said, "Samuel."

"Liza," he said. "I would like to speak with you alone."

Mother nodded to the girls, and they scattered to distant parts of the barn. Rebecca hid herself behind their cow and began to milk.

"Liza, will you not come home to me now?"

"Not unless you have something to say."

"I have something to say," he said.

"Then say on."

Peeking around the cow, Rebecca could see that he was throttling his hat, and she suspected the hat might never be the same again.

"There is order in the kingdom, Liza," he said. "A man presides in his own home."

Mother gazed at him, then picked up her sewing and began sticking her needle in with precise thrusts.

"Yes, husband. One must have order in the kingdom. You are the head of the family, and no one can take that away from you."

Father stared at her while her needle poked and the thread slid. From her hiding spot, Rebecca could see that Mother's fingers were perfectly poised.

Father lifted both arms straight out from his sides, then dropped them to his sides, smacking the crushed hat against his thigh. He was sweating as if the day were not cool.

"Do you want us all to starve?" he cried.

"I do not want you to starve."

"Well. Then. Do you want to break my heart?"

Mother's needle was stilled. Slowly she put down her hoop and stood up.

"I have no wish to break a heart that is so intimately connected to my own," she said. "But nor will I see a sister's heart broken, not only by her husband, but by all the men who knew and did nothing to protect her."

"I despise such behavior, but surely it cannot be my place to interfere. Let her come to us. A man's position as head of the home is God-given."

"Is it?" Mother said. Father took a step back. "If so, a

man's obligation to the happiness of his family is the reason it was given." She folded her hands across her waist and sighed. "And I have further to say, husband. If God has made you ruler over your own home, has it never passed your mind that I rebelled in my heart against this order every day? Perhaps other women retire their wills, take joy in a narrow stewardship. But not me, husband. Every decision you have made, without consulting me, for good or ill, I have had to forgive you for. Did you never know there are things about you that I find hard to bear? Your silence about anything that happens on the inside of you, your unnatural love of a field or a forest, the way you seek my counsel when you have already made up your mind, the way you ignore our daughter over the dinner conversation, or think you understand the work of a midwife because you have delivered a cow of a calf? The way everything about you inspires unreasonable love in me?"

The gentle delivery of her speech belied the content of it.

"I told myself as a young bride that I would wait for the right time to air my grievances, and now that time has come. There is nothing in our doctrine that excuses you."

He wrung his hat again. "You are right, Liza," he said.

"If you are given office, it is for the purpose of blessing and serving your people, your family, me. Your neighbor."

Rebecca could see that the skin beneath his beard was whiter than his whitest whiskers. She knew he was taking a beating.

He shook his head.

"I have said my fill," Mother said, and she seemed to sag

a little, like she did after she'd laundered and wrung out all the quilts.

Father looked down at his hat, surprised, it seemed, to see how badly he had mangled it. He put it on his head, and it sat limp and lopsided. Still, Rebecca thought he had never looked so handsome.

"I am grateful, Liza, that you have been honest with me, and I am sorry that the right time to speak your mind did not come sooner. I am guilty of all you say, and I wish to be a better man." He held out both his hands. "I will go to Sempel this very hour. Come back to our bed now, please."

Mother said, "There's one more thing."

"Name it," Father said.

"I want you to quit smoking," Mother said.

Father rocked on his feet a little. Rebecca heard Philemon gasp.

Father nodded and straightened his shoulders. "I will do it."

For a long moment they regarded each other, Father and Mother. Mother was so beautiful in that barn, so tall and straight and strong. Such a thing could a woman be. Mother God herself, Rebecca suspected, must stand eye to eye with Him, equal in glory. He would have no lesser being to enjoy eternity with.

Father picked up the rocking chair, and Mother glanced backward in the direction of her daughters. "Please bring my sewing, girls."

SEMPELS

"We'll go right away, won't we, Mother?" Rebecca asked while everyone was celebrating Mother's return to the house. "To the Sempels'?"

Even with all the trouble of Mother in the barn, she had worried about Sister Sempel.

"Yes," Mother said. "Ammon, get the wagon ready, please."

"I'll ride Tiny," Rebecca said.

Mother conferred with Father about something, and Rebecca went out to the barn, before Ammon.

Rebecca once again saw Sempel's spotty cow.

"I think you're going where I'm going," Rebecca said. She saddled Tiny, grabbed some alfalfa, put a rope around the neck of the patient cow, and began wrangling it toward its own barn.

At one point Rebecca stopped and looked back to see if her family was coming. What was taking them so long? Finally, when she was almost at the Sempel house, she saw them some way behind. She waited, still sitting on Tiny. She looked for Sempel in his fields or with his cattle, but she couldn't see him. Impatient, she went into the Sempels' yard, and when he didn't appear from the barn, she dismounted Tiny and let the cow go. She made her way cautiously to the front door and knocked.

"Sister Sempel, Mother is on her way. She'll be here any minute."

No answer.

She knocked on the door again. "It's me, Rebecca, Sister Sempel."

No one came to the door, so Rebecca peeked in and saw the woman sitting in the middle of a terrible mess. It looked as though someone had tried to break up or tear up everything in the house.

"Father and my brothers are coming, too, so you must pack your things right away," Rebecca said, stepping inside. "You will be safe now. Mother made sure."

"You leave the girl be, Pietr," Sister Sempel said, looking past Rebecca and into the open door.

Rebecca turned to see Sempel standing there.

She brushed past him and into the yard.

Sempel seemed surprised that Rebecca would walk right past him like that, as if a person needed permission to walk past him.

"There's my cow, with your rope around its neck. You must be stealing milk from it again. And now you are trespassing on my property. I know what's wrong with you," he said, following Rebecca into the yard, "and it's nothing a good beating won't fix. You still owe me for milk, and I'm going to take the price of it out of your hide right now."

He grabbed the whip from his horse's holster and struck her. Rebecca was so shocked, she felt no pain. The second time, she felt the whip on her back like a long, thin burn.

Sister Sempel cried and ran to Rebecca to shield her, and then Sempel used his whip on his wife. Rebecca could hear horses approaching. It would be over soon, it would be over soon... Sempel whipped his wife again and again, and his wife folded to the ground.

And then Sempel folded also—for someone had shot him.

Rebecca looked up. Mother was holding her 12-gauge shotgun.

Ammon quickly came to Rebecca.

"I'm all right," she said.

Mother's face was white as bleached sheets.

Father attended to Sempel, who cursed ferociously. He'd been shot close to the ankle and the leg bone was broken by it, Father said. He staunched the bleeding and splinted the leg, none too gently. The whole time Sempel was swearing that his wife was the source of all his troubles, and he was going to Fort Macleod to see a doctor and then the Mounties and then get as drunk as he'd like. Father got him his horse and all the while Sempel cursed Father and Mother and Rebecca and all the hosts of heaven.

They brought Sister Sempel home and it was decided that Ammon would take her to Lethbridge immediately. From there she would make her way to Toronto, where she had a maiden aunt her husband didn't know about. There she would be safe.

Once they were gone, Mother tended to Rebecca's welts. Later that day the Mounties from Fort Macleod showed up and Mother was invited to spend the night in their jail.

Father and Gideon went along with Mother until they left her in custody, and Rebecca later learned that Father then stayed behind to look for Sempel. He found him liquored up and smelling of his own vomit, having no stamina for drink. Father himself paid for Sempel to stay at the hotel and paid for him to have a bath and a shave. Afterward, he and Father had a long talk over dinner at the hotel, out of the hearing of others.

The next morning Rebecca and her brothers and sisters-in-law got up at dawn to meet Father and attend the hearing in Fort Macleod. Mother was taken out of jail like Lazarus out of the tomb—looking a little worn for it. Father was allowed to hold her hand as she stood before the judge. Her spine was straight, but her head was bowed. Philemon was weeping a little, Florence was erect and pale, their husbands' faces bloated a bit from wearing too-tight ties. Ammon looked as if he might spring out of his seat at any moment. Brother and Sister Card were in attendance. Rebecca had no idea how they had heard about Mother, but she was glad they were there.

"Mrs. Leavitt," the circuit judge said, "I know you to be a fine upstanding woman of your community, a skilled and dedicated midwife and nurse. I've been told in no uncertain terms by Mr. Card that it's a sin a woman of your character should spend a night in jail, never mind be sentenced. But the law must be upheld. I must ask, have you taken the law into your own hands and shot a man?"

"Sir, I did not take the law into my own hands."

"No?"

"No, sir."

"But I see before me a man on crutches"—he gestured to Sempel—"his leg broken, wounded by a bullet that came out of a gun you shot."

"Sir, I have not taken the law into my own hands for there is no law against a man beating his wife."

The judge looked around the courtroom as if someone else might provide an answer to that. "Well, I guess I knew that." He leaned back in his chair and made a sound as if he were weary of life. "It comes to this, Mrs. Leavitt: you made yourself judge, jury, and executioner, and shot a man in the leg. Can we agree to that?"

"I did not know what else to do, sir. He was whipping my daughter and his wife."

"Good lord, woman, what about Christian love and forgiveness?"

"Your Honor," Mother said, "I do love Pietr Sempel like the brother he should be, and I loved him even more once I'd shot him."

Rebecca looked at Father, and she didn't think a more admiring or devoted look could come shining out of a man's eyes. She wanted someone to look at her like that someday when she was old. She thought the judge must think her mother the most sensible creature in the world for saying that. But the judge looked down at Mother as if he'd like to tap her on the head with his gavel. Finally he closed his eyes and shook his head.

"Ma'am, I'm sorry to say that I'm going to have to sentence you for what you've done."

"Yes, sir. I'm sorry, too, sir," Mother said meekly. Her shoulders curled over.

Rebecca started to rise, to speak, to cry out, but Gideon put his hand before her and shook his head. How could Father be silent and allow his wife, who was not even a little lower than the angels, to go to jail? At least without speaking up?

Just then Brother Sempel stood up, leaning on a cane and puffing out his chest importantly. "Judge, I have something to say."

"What is it, Sempel?" The judge was decidedly less patient with Sempel than with Mother.

"I'm dropping the charges, Your Honor."

"What?" the judge said.

"What?" Mother said.

"In my painful delirium, I thought Mrs. Leavitt had shot me o' purpose, when in fact it was an accident."

"But she confessed!" the judge said.

"Her word against mine," Sempel said.

The judge looked at Mother and Sempel, shook his head, and made a grunting sound.

"I have a long way to go to my next stop, and it promises to be a hot day. Ladies and gentlemen, case dismissed." His gavel came down.

Rebecca helped Mother onto the wagon and jumped in after. Mother looked less like a prisoner and more like a queen.

Sempel approached Father. "Well?" he said to Father.

Father arranged the reins and ignored him.

"You said if I dropped the charges you would tell me where my wife went!"

"I said that."

"And so?"

"I have no intention of telling you where your wife went, Sempel. Good day."

As the wagon pulled away, Mother and Father sat high up on the wagon seat and held their heads high. Mother had shot a man. Father had lied. And yet somehow they were Samuel and Eliza Leavitt still. Rebecca felt the mountains had been tipped upside down, balancing on their snowy tips, their roots floating up like ribbons toward the clouds. It was not such a bad feeling.

COBY

I n a matter of days, Brother Sempel put his outfit up for
sale at great discount and arranged for the land agent
to dispose of his land and cattle. Then he left for Missouri.
Through a third party, Father acquired the spotty cow for
Rebecca. He felt she'd earned it, and now the spotty cow ate
the hay because it was her hay. Best of all, Florence and Zach
were expecting a baby. Rebecca thought Philemon might be
sad and tried to comfort her, but Philemon shared a secret
with Rebecca: she might be expecting one of her own. It was
still too early to tell even Gideon, but not her sister.

Rebecca was happy. She was. But she allowed herself
to be sad in the hayloft whenever hay harvesting and the
last-minute bottling would allow. She was sad because
Ammon was sad about LaRue, and, yes, when she dared to
face it, sad because of her land.

She had started a new quilt for Coby. The one she had
started so long ago and never finished had been washed
away in the flood. She used scraps Philemon and Florence
donated for the project. When it was done, Rebecca was
a better quilter than when she had begun, for Mother had
looked over her work and made sure she did it right, and
her sisters helped her. She could have given it to Coby the

next time he came for Sunday dinner, but she told herself she couldn't wait—she wanted to surprise him with it now.

She took it to his house, and when she saw he wasn't home she let herself in and laid it on his bed herself. She was admiring it and smoothing it out when he returned.

She felt again how much space he took up in his cabin.

"I had to start a new quilt for you because of the flood, but now I've finished."

He stepped closer to look. "It's fine, Rebecca," he said, and she could tell he meant it.

"It'll be warm," she said. "And sturdy. It'll outlast you. Nine stiches to the inch... Only Radonna can do better, as she would tell you herself."

"Why are you so hard on her?" he asked.

"Me? Hard on her?"

"She's unhappy here, you know. She didn't want to come to the Territories, but her father made her come. She's tried to make the best of it, having parties and such, but she doesn't belong in a place like this. And then along comes Levi and she's happy for the first time, and there's you coming between them."

Rebecca sputtered, and then said, "You don't know how she feels about Levi. She's just—she's probably just flirting with him to get back at me."

"Is she?"

"Yes. And you don't know how Levi feels about her... or about me... You don't know anything."

"I know you. And I'm the only one who will tell you the truth."

"Well," she said.

He sat down on the bed, still looking at her, and put his hand on the quilt. It was such a nothing gesture, but it felt like something. Was he inviting her to sit beside him? Her knees almost buckled.

"I have an idea, Coby, and maybe you can help. What if we went looking for Joe Cosley's ring tomorrow, if the weather's as fine as it's been?"

"Lots of people have tried to find the ring, and nobody has," Coby said.

"Lots of people is not us."

He smiled at that. "True."

"Let's make it a fishing trip and we'll hike around and see what we see. Fall is the best time of year for fishing."

"Just us?" he asked.

She stood mute for a moment.

"I'll let Minnie know," she said, "and she'll let Kit know, and he'll let Levi know, and by morning we'll have a party of us. And I'll — I'll even make sure Radonna is invited."

"Oh," he said. "Oh, sure. Yes, tell the others."

"But not about the ring. I want to find it myself, if it's there."

They gathered at Rebecca's before the sun was up but the sky was tender. Rebecca had made fried-egg sandwiches for everyone to eat in the saddle.

"Look at that Chinook arch," Loyal said.

"It's going to be beautiful," Minnie said, calming her horse. Even the horses were anxious to be going.

Nobody asked about Ammon, which meant they knew better than to ask, which both annoyed and satisfied Rebecca. Ammon worked obsessively these days anyway, and when he wasn't working, he hid in his room reading and rereading the secret notes that LaRue smuggled to him and writing his own back to her. Rebecca knew from little things Ammon said that LaRue might be wearing her father down. And should it come to it, they were still making plans to run away when the baby was born at the end of the year.

Radonna didn't like fishing or hiking, but when she heard Levi was coming, she went along with it. She was an excellent horsewoman and Levi rode beside her. Rebecca did her best not to be unseated by Tiny, and not to notice the untidy mane of Coby's Blackfoot pony. Most of the way there, when she wasn't talking and laughing with Coby and the others, she kept an eye on Radonna and Levi talking together. Did he really care for Radonna? They would make a handsome couple, she had to admit. But what about the times he showed up just as her family was sitting down to dinner? What about that horse Levi had given to her father, and the hours he spent helping to build the new house? Hadn't that been for her? What about the gallant little attentions he paid her at the cook line and elsewhere, and which she couldn't help encouraging? He had said he was proud of Rebecca for wanting to buy land—Coby had never said as much.

They arrived at the lake midmorning, starving and cold. It was a glorious fall day, but the wind blew the birds around and whipped the trees, and little whitecaps tumbled on Waterton Lake. The wind always blew, and was always part of the beauty. On the other side of the lake, there were no banks, just the mountains rising straight up out of the water, and the formidable timber that stretched endlessly into Montana. The forest here was not like the woods of England, which could house a band of merry thieves, or so Mother had told her. A forest here was dark and close and wild and dangerous, and "merry" could never describe it. You could walk into the forests here and never find your way out again. That, Rebecca thought, was a true forest.

Rebecca brought fresh bread to the picnic, Minnie and Lyla brought apples from British Columbia and newly dug carrots. Radonna brought a box of cookies and cupcakes, and the men quickly caught enough fish for a good fry-up.

Radonna sat beside Levi as they ate. Rebecca admired how she ate so daintily, and how carefully she listened to every word Levi said. He was easy enough to listen to— gallant, intelligent, a little daring. Next to him, Coby said little, although when he did speak, he made them laugh.

When they'd eaten Rebecca said, "Let's hike up."

The group looked up to the top of the mountain. Its lower slopes were dressed in lodgepole pine, spruce and birch, except where avalanches had gouged out the trees and earth in long cuts.

Minnie said, "I bet the girls could beat the boys to the top."

Coby said, "There'll be bears up there this time of year, so everyone stay together."

Levi grinned and said, "Bears. I wouldn't worry, Coby."

"I won't worry if we stay together," Coby said.

"Bears don't hurt anybody," Levi said.

Rebecca knew that wasn't true. She'd known of two people who died of bear. But she didn't speak up. She didn't want anyone to think her afraid, even though Coby didn't seem to mind.

"I think I'll stay close to you anyway, Levi," Radonna said.

Levi didn't seem to mind if Radonna was worried about bears.

Kit reached up to ruffle Coby's hair. It was a reach indeed, for Coby's hair was at the top of a tall man. "Don't worry, I'll protect you," Kit said.

Coby smiled like the good sport he was.

They secured the horses near grass and water, and followed a foot trail that cut through the trees and bushes. The trail led around the north side of the mountain and rose by switchbacks to a great height. Every so often they got a glimpse of the falls cascading down the mountains, but as they climbed, the underbrush became denser and much of the fun was gone out of it. Rebecca, and Coby, too, she could tell, kept an eye open for any tree with the initials JC carved into it, or for a ring dangling from a branch.

After a couple of hours, the others began to complain about pinching shoes and weary feet, but Rebecca urged them on until finally they became silent with their misery. They shed their jackets and tied them around their waists as the day warmed.

When the trees began to thin and they emerged into an alpine meadow, they stopped. They took off their shoes and boots and moaned, but Coby was silent, reverent, looking at the view.

"Look at that," Coby said. "You can live out your life in a place like this and not be sorry."

Surely it was a view of heaven, Rebecca thought: the arêtes, sharp spires brittle and dry against the blue-wet sky;

197

the cirques scooped out of the mountains, round and big enough to hold a moon; the great sweeps of alpine meadow and the glacier ice above. Below them was a herd of bighorn sheep, grazing on a mountain meadow. The bighorn didn't mind the wind and the winters, for they burned good mountain grass in their bellies.

Farther down the slopes were black pine on the high ridges, then down and down to the lakes, full of pure pressed-down glacier water. From there they could see across the prairie, south to Montana. More important, she could see her Sitting Rock. Of course, it wasn't her Sitting Rock at all, and never would be. Unless she found Joe's ring.

"This view is darn beautiful," Loyal said.

The others looked at Rebecca, waiting for her to chide him for swearing.

But she was thinking in that moment that if anything in the world deserved a swear it was for that distant tor. She would spend her swears all in one place for it.

"It is," she said. "It's bloody damn stupid beautiful."

Levi laughed. Coby nodded.

"We'd best get down if we're going to be home by dark," Radonna said.

"Let's go a different way down to the lake," Rebecca said.

"The trail is rougher that way," Levi said.

"And there's more likelihood of bears," Coby said.

"I'm not going that way," said Minnie.

"Nor me," said Lyla. "My feet are wore out. I'm going the easy way."

"We should stay together, whatever way we go," said Coby.

"You're looking for Joe Cosley's ring, aren't you, Rebecca," Radonna said. She laughed shortly.

Everyone looked at Rebecca as if she'd forgotten to tell them all the rules of the game. Rebecca couldn't think of anything to say for a moment, and then, "What if I am?" Rebecca said. "Aren't you looking for a ring yourself?"

The trees stopped shushing in that moment, so the whole world could hear what had just come out of her mouth.

Radonna looked at her fingers, as if they betrayed her by not having a ring on one of them.

Levi almost always looked amused, as if he thought the world were the funniest thing. But now he only looked uncomfortable.

"Well, I'm taking the other trail down," Rebecca said, standing and walking away from the group.

Coby followed.

For a long time they walked and didn't talk. Rebecca looked for a bit of starlight trapped in a tree, but her heart wasn't in it now, as it had been on the way up.

Finally she said, "Coby, why can't I be good?"

After a long silence he said, "Why can't we all?"

"You are good."

He shook his head and sighed. "It's goodness in you to see it in others, Reb."

"It's just like you to say that." Why did all the trees refuse to have diamonds in them? "I shall have to apologize to Radonna."

"Yes," he said.

"It will be hard."

"Yes," he said.

"Don't you care?"

"Yes," he said.

She thought about how she might apologize and still keep her pride. But sometimes pride had to go, there were no two ways around it.

This was what she was thinking when she heard a loud, deep *harrumph*.

A deep-bellied, indignant grunt.

A warning.

A bear.

She turned her head ever so slowly. It wasn't just a bear. It was a grizzly bear. A mama grizzly bear.

With a cub.

Coby took her hand. "Be still, Reb. Don't look her in the eye."

Rebecca lowered her eyes.

"Don't move a muscle," he said. "And don't be afraid. They can smell fear."

She knew she must smell like a big ol' loaf of fear, a big rank roast of fear. She knew, and she knew that bear knew, that her fear was just begging that mama bear to eat her up.

The bear was as big as two bulls put together. She huffed again. Rebecca could hear the cub scrambling around its mother. In her side vision she saw the grizzly swing her massive head.

"Co-by!" she whispered.

She knew if they'd come between the mama and her cub, she'd already be dead. Lord, she prayed, I never wanted to die by bear. She thought of all the stories she'd heard. The worst one was of a bear that took someone's head off with a single swipe of its plate-sized paw. She most particularly didn't want to have to wander about on resurrection morning looking for her head.

"Shh...," Coby whispered. "They're leaving now."

The mama bear blew out some air and lumbered away a few steps. She looked back, as if she weren't sure she was done with them.

"Don't move yet," Coby whispered.

Rebecca knew she couldn't move anyway. After what seemed a long time, she heard the bears well away from her in the underbrush. Still, Rebecca knew she would never move again. Never again.

"We're safe now, Rebecca. Are you okay?"

"I'm okay," she said. Her knees buckled, and she went down.

"You did everything right," he said, kneeling beside her. "You never moved and you kept your eyes lowered and you did good."

"I never wanted to die by bear, Coby. What if they take a bite out of you in a place that doesn't kill you? They don't start with heads, you know, unless it's just to swipe it off and sometimes they just mess you up and don't eat you at all, they bite you and they don't like the taste of you and there you are with a bite out of you, the soft important parts of you—you need those parts, Coby, and the bear she just walks away—and it's a big waste—you're just a big waste —or sometimes they drag your body away and bury you so you can get rotten because they like their meat better that way, and nobody ever finds you and you don't get a burial." She took a deep breath. "You were right to worry about bears, Coby. And I'm sorry I made us go this way."

"Being right's nothing so long as you're okay."

She lay back on the forest floor and stared up, through the branches, to the late-afternoon sky. How could it still be light? Hadn't hours and hours passed, waiting for the bears to go away? Her brain must be addled.

"Land, that mama bear was something, wasn't she, Coby?" she said at last.

He collapsed beside her and stared up at the sky. "She was. Never seen one that big before."

"Thank you, Coby."

"Why?"

"For—for—I don't know. Everything."

He propped himself on one elbow and looked at her. She didn't move. She let him look. She would let him look and look at her. He could get up as close as he wanted. He could look right into her soul if he wanted, for being so brave and sensible, for being Coby in every way.

The muscles in his arms were veined and quivering. He was gulping up all her air, staring at her mouth like he wanted to suck all the breath out of her. She felt loose in the joints, utterly still, the way a cornered animal goes just before the kill.

"Do you want me to kiss you, Rebecca?"

Yes, she thought.

No, she thought.

Who are you? she wanted to say. You're just Coby. But then she wanted to say, whatever you are asking of me, Coby, whatever it is…

He stood up, quick, silent, and the light he'd been blocking blinded her.

They walked in silence.

All the rest of the way down, Coby was quiet, but not in an unkind way. Instead of looking for the ring, she looked at Coby. She felt all his dimensions in a way she hadn't noticed before, the width of his shoulders, and the length of his arms, and the thickness of his thighs. She was aware of her distance from him, a hand's breadth, an arm's length, almost touching. She was aware of how tanned his neck was, and his arms and face, and how he breathed and how his foot trod the ground, and his hands — how had she never seen how his hands were before: large and angular and rough and brown and beautiful. She forgot to think about woods with grizzlies and rings in them, because she thought about woods with Coby in them.

They were nearing the bottom when Coby stopped cold on the trail near a ridge. He gazed past a tree on the ridge, and then slowly walked toward it.

"What is it?" she asked, following. Below stretched a green meadow.

"Look!" he whispered.

Rebecca looked and saw a beautiful animal, graceful and fine-limbed and handsome as a deer, but bigger, and muscled as a moose.

"What is it?" she whispered.

"That," Coby said, "is a miracle." He knelt in the grass.

"A miracle?"

"That there is an elk."

She knelt beside him. After a time, four more elk

ventured out of the timber and into the meadow. They were the most powerful yet graceful animals she had ever seen.

"Don't tell anyone," Coby said. "This is just for you and me."

"We've got to tell, Coby. If we don't, nobody will know you were right about the elk coming back."

"That's as will be," he said.

"But how can you stand it? Don't you like to be right?"

"You know about them," he said. "That's good enough for me."

"But I don't count."

"You're all what counts," he said.

She felt peaceful in her whole being, watching the elk, thinking about Coby saying what he'd just said.

Coby smiled. "Right now I feel like I'll never be sad again."

"Have you been sad?" she asked.

"Course I've been sad. Everybody's been sad."

"Well, don't tell me so," she said. "I can't bear it."

He watched the elk with what could be nothing less than joy.

"Yes, please," she said.

He looked at her.

"I mean, to the kiss," she said. "Yes, please."

Then his mouth was on hers, and right then and there she and Coby invented kissing. He kissed her and kissed her again, and she let him and let him. Whatever he wanted, the answer was yes.

Her spine bloomed into flame, until all that was left was light on bone.

He stopped, trying to get his breath.

"Do it again," she said.

"Better not," he said.

The others had been waiting when she and Coby arrived back at the lake, and on seeing them, they began saddling up to go home. Neither she nor Coby said a thing to the others about the bear or the elk; they were secrets for only them to know. The others complained about their blisters, but Rebecca and Coby were quiet.

Coby stayed close to her, but casually, not for anyone else to see. She didn't speak to him, but she felt a strange stillness inside her. Coby was tall, but it was the height of something inside him she was seeing now, the way he was taller than teasing, the way he never had to tell other people he had been right. She liked being the only one to know him that way. She liked knowing the forest had a diamond in it, and she liked knowing that the world had a Coby in it. If only it was a world that had a girl with her very own land in it.

On the way home, she noticed that Levi avoided riding beside Radonna. He talked and laughed as usual, and Radonna did as well, but they didn't speak to each other specifically the whole ride home. Rebecca thought she might have used up all her courage on that bear, but she made herself sidle up to Radonna when they were almost at the point of parting.

"Radonna, I want to say — I want to say I'm sorry — "

"For what?" Radonna said sharply. She smiled her most forkish smile, then kicked her horse and galloped off toward home. She waved a hand at everyone who called goodbye, but she didn't look back.

GRIPPE

Philemon put down her knitting and stood as soon as Rebecca walked in. Rebecca was glad it was Philemon and not Mother, because she wouldn't have to talk, she could just let Philemon do all the work of conversation. All Rebecca wanted to do was think about Coby and that kiss.

"Mother Leavitt wanted me to tell you that she's gone to the Allens'. They've got the grippe."

The news went down like cold water on a cold day. Rebecca knew the grippe could rage through the country-side, more devastating than a tornado. Little could be done to relieve the grippe, and certainly nothing could be done to cure it. Some years the grippe came in not much worse than a chest cold. Other years it caused scorching fevers and pneumonia and delirium and death. Often it was the very old and the very young who succumbed, but some-times it was those in their prime. There was no one to blame but God, which challenged one's loyalty, Rebecca thought, even knowing that death had been part of the bargain.

"I'm going to help Mother," Rebecca said, and it didn't even surprise her that she'd said it.

At first she worked at her mother's side, but once she had learned what to do, and when family after family began to come down with it, she was sent to nurse them on her own. She made onion poultices and mustard plasters, and saturated cheesecloth in eucalyptus. She spooned sulfur-and-molasses tea and broth into the mouths of the sick. There was niter for fever. She emptied chamber pots and boiled handkerchiefs and milked people's lonesome cows.

Sister Card and other sisters also nursed the sick. For some, nothing could be done. The life in them unspooled: backward they went from strong to helpless, backward from stoic courage to childlike whimpering and no control of their bowels, backward to blind infancy, backward to blue and breathless like a newborn just out of the womb. The first time it happened, Rebecca folded Sister Wixom in her arms and sang to her and held her until she was gone. "Sister," she said when the woman stopped breathing, "sister, sister."

She rode to Mother and told her that Sister Wixom had died, died in her very arms, and when she said Sister Wixom, when she said the word *sister*, she meant it, oh, she meant it.

She thought Mother would hold her and comfort her, but she said, "You are healthy?"

"My heart is sick."

"Then you must continue as you've begun. You can't go home now, Rebecca, and take it to Father and the rest. How is Brother Wixom?"

"He is up now, and taking care of the children."

"Someone is needed at Johnsons', for the whole family has just come down with it."

Mother went back to work, nursing a family of eight, and Rebecca got on her horse and rode to Johnsons'.

Every person was a surprise, she was learning. Every soul never had its copy. Each one a world to itself, a world of that soul's making, and when that soul was gone, a whole world ended. It didn't matter if they started out old or ugly or cranky; by the end of it they were sweet and soft beyond bearing. She held the dying, each one a world, and she loved the life of that solitary world, that single bit of holy flame that birthed itself back to God. She'd thought it strange, when nursing the sick, that just when life was all but gone, just at the moment when things seemed most unfair, that was when they loved God most. Why? she had wondered. What did they see on that precipice? What view? What new world, new understanding? How did they, in the end, hand over life so simply? A breath not breathed, and peace.

Sometimes Mother came to relieve Rebecca, to let her sleep, though she wondered if there was anyone to give Mother similar relief. Rebecca asked Mother why she didn't get sick, and she answered that it was because she went so often into the house of the sick, the grippe had given up on her. Rebecca decided that if stubbornness was a preventative, that explained why she didn't get sick herself.

Sometimes Levi or Coby or Ammon appeared, bringing wood or coal or to do chores, but they never came inside for fear of Mother's wrath. As the church sisters healed, they went out to help as well. Those who couldn't help sent soup and bread.

But they were only visitors to Rebecca's real world, which now was filled with spirits, the deathbed room crowded with spirits, like a family reunion waiting for the honored guest to arrive. She felt the spirits around her whispering, and the dying said the names of the dead, and then it was over and the house was empty of all but the living.

Sister Yardley, when she sickened, sang in her delirium, and it was sweet angel tones that came out of her mouth. She smiled as if she'd been singing with angels, as if she'd been given her dream come true, and she began to be well.

Old Solomon Mack, who never strung more than a dozen words together, began telling Rebecca stories about princes and dragons and great battles, and Rebecca told him he must battle the grippe and live to tell the end. He smiled and said he thought he would. And he did. When he learned, however, that his brother had died, he became more silent than ever. Brother Minder got well and said of Rebecca, "There ain't no girl with a better heart than you, dear." Sister Shepherd, when she recovered, said to Rebecca that she was a miracle. Rebecca loved them all.

One time Rebecca prayed away all her future visits with God, or all the ones she hoped for at the Sitting Rock, if only he would come and sit with little Fanon and make her better. But he did not come, and Fanon died, and her father, when he guessed, closed his eyes and went after her. Rebecca nursed Fanon's mother back to health, or at least to physical health. If she ever smiled again, Rebecca was not witness to it. Fanon's uncle said it all seemed unbecoming of a merciful creator, and Rebecca seemed to have forgotten the answer to that, if she'd ever had one.

One man brought bread to the door of the sick, and Rebecca took it gratefully until the man said, "I thank the Lord that all in my family have been blessed to avoid this plague, and we are all well." Rebecca couldn't say why that made her want to slap him, to want him to take his blessed self out of her sight and off to his own private heaven where the good do not suffer. He and his blessed family would be alone in heaven, wondering aloud why, but secretly pleased to suspect that they must be more special and loved than the rest of God's children. But no, she must not think critically, even of this man. She took the bread and loved him by saying, "Good brother, do shut up."

Gradually, fewer families came down with it, and Mother had begun to hope it was all but over when Rebecca got the news that LaRue's family needed help. The boys were coming down with it one by one, taking turns. But when baby Abigail came down with it, she died within a few hours of the onset of her fever. Sister Fletcher was too ill to cry out for her, and Brother Fletcher turned his face to the wall and wept and coughed until he was sick to his stomach. Now LaRue, who'd been caring for all of them, was sick.

Rebecca came and cared for them. LaRue couldn't sit up long, but she obediently sipped water and broth and ate soft eggs and teaspoons of jam. "For the baby," Rebecca would say, and LaRue would try. Her parents soon passed the most dangerous stage, but they would be a while recuperating.

"Did she suffer?" Rebecca asked, meaning of course LaRue's baby sister.

"She fell asleep and didn't wake up," LaRue said.

"LaRue," Rebecca said, "I sat on a rock with God."

LaRue searched her face. "I know you would never lie just to give me false comfort."

"I would not."

"We shall not speak of it again. These things are to be kept in the heart."

"Yes," Rebecca said. "And you are my heart."

Ammon came to chop wood and help with the livestock, having heard Brother Fletcher was down.

"Now see here, brother," Rebecca said when he came to the door. "You go take care of this farm. You get that hay in. You do the chores and fix the fencing and muck out the chicken coop and the barn better than Brother Fletcher ever did. You do it until he is well enough to chase you off his property, and maybe he won't."

"How is LaRue?"

"She's strong."

He nodded. "Tell her —"

"I will."

And so Ammon worked. He worked all day and into the evenings. He got his brothers to help, too. He fixed the fencing and repaired the corral. He mucked out the chicken coop and shoveled out the barn and polished the harness. He chopped wood and stacked it against the house. He worked and worked, and once, when Rebecca was looking out the window while washing bedding, she saw him kneeling in a field, as Father was wont to do.

Mother came to make sure Rebecca was holding up and to tell her that no one new had come down with it since the Fletchers, which was good news among the bad.

The day after Mother gave her the news, just when Rebecca thought she must perish of exhaustion, Radonna came to the door in an old gray dress and said, "I've come to help. I had a mild case of it, so they say I'm safe from it now. Put me to work."

"Here," Rebecca said, handing her a rag. "You can clean up the floor by Ormus's bed. And when you're done that, there is bedding to be washed." Rebecca didn't tell her the state of the bedding—best not to deal with some afflictions before they presented themselves.

Together Rebecca and Radonna worked. Radonna sang to the little boys and rocked them in her arms. Rebecca thought she had never seen Radonna so beautiful, but she wouldn't tell her so.

When they had a few moments, Rebecca said, "I wish to be friends now, Radonna."

Radonna said, "We shall, but anyway we are more than friends. We are sisters."

"And so we are," Rebecca said.

The Fletcher family began to recover, and one day Brother Fletcher found the strength to get out of his sick-bed to take a look at his farm. Rebecca followed him out the door.

He walked like an old man to the barn and stared around at it—everything clean and orderly, and the horses polished up like show horses. The hay was fragrant and bountiful in the loft.

Ammon came riding in from checking on the livestock.

He dismounted and he and Brother Fletcher looked at each other across a bit of a distance.

"It's Ammon as did all the work," Rebecca said.

"I had some help," Ammon said.

Brother Fletcher said, "Aren't you scared to be on my land, young man?"

"Yes, sir."

"Well, I'll tell you something, Ammon," Brother Fletcher said in a different kind of voice. "I was scared. The whole time I was sick, when I was in my right mind, I was scared that I was going to leave my family without someone to provide for them, and that I was going to meet my God with a cold and unforgiving heart. Now, my daughter is still in her bed, and I don't think she'll get well until she sees you. So you'd best go to her."

Ammon seemed to be going over this speech as if to be sure he had understood it.

"Git!"

"Yes, sir!"

Ammon got.

Day after day, no new sick were reported, and Mother said it was over. They went home. Father looked thin, though Philemon and Florence had done their best to cook and care for him. Father kissed his wife in front of everyone.

Then he turned to Rebecca and said, "You did good, my brave daughter."

This from a man who was highly suspicious of the effects of praise on the young soul.

Rebecca replied, "I wouldn't take a million dollars for this past time, Father, and I wouldn't give you two cents for another just like it."

Funerals were held, and people came fasting, hungry and heartbroken. Those who had lost loved ones awakened to a new world, one that was less kind than the old one. But they had lived and they would live.

Rebecca had decided, while she spoon-fed broth and emptied chamber pots and applied poultices, that people were miracles. They woke up each day swimming in their sorrows and fears and got up and braved the day and cared for their little ones and had a thought for others. They planted the land and babied their crops so they could live. They hurt and they yearned and they hoped, and nobody could stop them. God never came, and they prayed. He took their babies away, and they worshipped. They suffered, and they served. They were beautiful as an idea, and they were beautiful in the particular. And Rebecca could never unknow it.

Ammon and LaRue were married at the Leavitts' house with only their families and Coby and Levi in attendance. There was neither wedding breakfast nor wedding dress, but Ammon and LaRue seemed not to mind or even to notice. LaRue got busy turning her little house into a perfect nest, for she knew how to work all the livelong day, and their baby would arrive very soon. LaRue had become Rebecca's sister in deed. She was grateful to Ammon for this one good act of eternal import.

The Sunday after they were married, which was the first Sunday that people felt safe to attend church again, LaRue and Ammon went to church on their own, as did Gideon with Philemon and Zach with Florence. All the family waited and entered together, with LaRue in the middle. It was the first LaRue had been seen at church since May. All eyes were upon her and Ammon. They could have guessed what people may have been saying, or at least thinking about them. But before they got to the pew, LaRue stopped beside Sister Shuling, put her hand on her shoulder, and said softly, "How did your roses fare this year, Sister Shuling?"

Sister Shuling put her hand over LaRue's and said, "Well, dear, and come summer I'll have cuttings for you for your little home."

LaRue stopped beside Sister Doxie as well. "How is your star quilt, sister?" she asked.

"It turned out beautifully, LaRue, and it will make a wonderful wedding gift for you."

That evening, bundled against the cold, Rebecca rode to the tor—the first time since she'd given her money to her parents.

She felt the sadness all over again, that she wouldn't have her land. Coby had been seen at the land office; Gideon had told her gently. Of course, his preemption rights were expiring, and he had to buy the land now or lose his right to buy it. He would be putting his ten dollars down on the land she had longed for. Land, she thought. It never broke your heart in all the thousand ways a heart could be broken. It just sat there and let you satisfy yourself in its dimensions, let you gaze at it and name it and never asked a thing of you. But no, that wasn't right. It asked a very great deal of her father and her brothers and her people. This land, it had to be negotiated with every day, as if it were a small god that wanted to be served, appeased, with no promise of rewarding the faithful. What had she been thinking, anyway? You couldn't live on scenery. Father had been right about that. But then, she thought, she couldn't live without it, either.

All her hoping had come out of love. Oh, she loved this place. She wanted the buffalo grass to live, in case a buffalo ever wandered out of her dreams and on by.

She could hear Coby coming up, heard his steps coming closer.

But then it wasn't Coby. It was Levi.

"Your mother told me where I could probably find you," he said. "May I?"

She nodded, and he sat beside her on the rock.

Levi.

He talked about the grippe and the sorrows of it.

He talked about his horse ranch and how well it was doing.

He talked about perhaps selling out and starting again somewhere south, somewhere that had better weather in the winter. She nodded and murmured and continued to gaze at the mountains while he talked.

He fell silent for a time.

He took off his hat and raked through his hair with his fingers. It was a fine head of hair.

She wished she could tell him that this rock he was sitting on, oh so casually, so loosely and comfortably, as he was loose and comfortable everywhere, was a place for watching sunsets, a place you came where you could watch the sunset all alone and yet never be alone.

"Levi," she said slowly and carefully, "isn't this a place where God would come to sit and look out and take his rest?"

He laughed softly, then sobered when she glanced at him. He smoothed his mustache.

"Don't you think," he said, "that God would go to many places before he came here?"

She was silent for a time, and then, "Perhaps he did."

"May I speak seriously for a moment, Rebecca? I have come to ask —"

He gripped his knees. "It's just that . . . I've watched you over the past year, and I've come to admire you, Rebecca — very much, really. And I would like to court you." He took her hands in both of his and kissed them.

Well.

There was once a time when she would hardly have dared dream of a moment like this.

She did love him, in a way, in one of the ways of loving. He was a good man, but did she see the world the way he saw the world? If she tied her life to his, they would look out the same window every day, and every day he would explain to her what he saw. He would be patient. And one day, either out of weariness or out of compassion or on a whim, she would say, "Yes, I see what you see."

But Coby — he saw an elk, and she had seen it, too, and they both knew it had been a miracle. For right or wrong, she never had to struggle to see what Coby saw, or if she did, she ended by being glad of it. She never had to forget herself.

"I'm sorry, Levi," she said.

He looked surprised. She had never seen him look surprised before; he looked completely different when he was surprised. He let go of her hands.

"Are you rejecting me, then, Rebecca?"

"I have saved you many griefs by doing so," she said.

He laughed, one short cough of a laugh, and then he

217

coughed some real coughs. After it stopped, he said, "There is no one like you in the world, Rebecca Leavitt."

"And every day the world is grateful," she said.

"I—I am suddenly not feeling well," he said. "I hope we can continue this conversation at a later time."

He stood and walked away.

The next day she heard that Levi had gone down with the grippe, surprising everyone, for they had assumed it was done with. Rebecca determined she would go to him the next morning, no matter how awkward, but the next morning she also came down with the grippe, down and down and down.

She was sick in every part of her body: her hair, her toes, her eyeballs. She had visions, ordinary visions, not of heaven but of home, which seemed far away: Ammon weeping by her bed, Father sitting and praying by her bed in the deep night, Gideon pressing a cold cloth to her head, Zach reading her the dear book, their beautiful wives singing to her, bathing her, telling her they loved her and she must get well. LaRue, wearing a halo on the back of her head like a shiny little bonnet, was as much with her as Mother was. Where LaRue touched her, Rebecca felt cool. When LaRue sang to her, she slept. Coby, too, might have been there, placing his hands on her head, commanding her to live. She might have dreamed him.

At some point, Rebecca became too sick to care if she cried. Her chest burned, her head was filled with a pain as if little horns had been torn from her skull and caustic rubbed into the holes. She was a small animal in the jaws of a wolf: shaken, limp, crushed. She opened her eyes once and looked at her fingers beside her on the pillow. Poor fingers, she thought, you are so sick…I never thought fingers could be so sick.

Mother tormented her by spooning water and broth and herb tea into her mouth. She tormented her with hot plasters on her chest and cool cloths on her head. She tormented her by changing her bedclothes and in general not letting her forget that she was not allowed to die. Once she had a convulsion, Father told her later, and Mother made Father hold her tongue so she wouldn't swallow it. Father said later it was the only time he'd been able to control his daughter's tongue.

She knew how easy it would be to simply roll out of her body and get up and walk away. Her body could barely hold her in—it had always been that way, she knew now—just a wet, fleshy coat that could be shrugged off in a moment, so easily discarded. She hadn't known before, but now she knew.

Her fingernails fell off and her skin peeled. Mother slathered her in precious olive oil, holy oil, oil set aside for the blessing of the sick. She felt her father's and her brothers' hands upon her head, pressing her back into her body, saying, you shall live. Those hands said, our lives would be a sorrow to us forever without you in it. She had a vision of Coby by her bed saying, that's enough, Rebecca, time to get better now. One didn't resist that much earnest priesthood. She would have to stay.

One day she woke up and asked for a poached egg.

The day after that she sat up for a few minutes on her own and asked for soup.

The next day, she stood up, and, with Mother's help, used the chamber pot and ate bread and sat in a chair.

And the day after that, Mother told her that Levi had died.

THE SIT

Rebecca got dressed. Her clothes felt strange upon her skin.

Father took her for a wagon ride, bundled up against the cold, to see the canal, all done now. Along the way he spoke about nothing and everything and asked her opinion about things.

"So what do you think of that?" he asked her when they came to the canal.

Canals were the human versions of rivers, she supposed, with none of the ferocious beauty of mountain streams and waterfalls, none of the deep and cold and old of the mountain lakes. Canals were straight, sluggish things, and she hated them.

"I hate it," she said.

Father nodded. "So do I," he said.

They looked at each other and smiled. It would be their secret.

When they got home, Rebecca said she was going to saddle up Tiny.

"Where are you going?" Mother asked. "You should rest now."

"I won't be long," she answered.

Rebecca was exhausted by the time she got the horse

saddled. But Tiny was good, as if he'd missed her, as if he knew she was fragile, and he didn't make her work at all.

At Radonna's, Rebecca dismounted and stood, arms at her sides, resting her head for a few moments on Tiny's flank.

"Rebecca."

She turned. For a moment, Rebecca thought she had made a mistake. For a moment, she thought this could not be Radonna at all. Radonna's face was always quick and her eyes chatty. This girl's face was immobile, her eyes puffy and silent. Radonna had a dozen different ways to smile. This girl looked as if she had never smiled.

The horse grunted and shook his head.

"Levi," Radonna said. "The grippe..." Her throat seemed to close over those words.

"I know," Rebecca said. How she wished she didn't know. "I came to you because I — I know what you have lost."

Rebecca thought she could stand one more minute if she used every muscle. Stand up, she told her muscles. Stand, I tell you. Lift your head. Look her in the eye, see her sorrow.

"We might have been married if he had not had doubts...because of you. I hate you for that."

"Yes," Rebecca said.

"I loved him. And he loved me."

"Yes," Rebecca said. Face the truth, she told herself. You think you can see the other side of a thing? Here is the other side of the thing: You have had imagination only for yourself. You had no imagination for Radonna and how she felt.

Radonna rushed toward her — to strike her? But Rebecca

stepped toward her and wrapped her arms around her. Radonna wept in her arms, and Rebecca's muscles held the two of them up while she did. Radonna's mother came out and guided them into the kitchen and warmed some milk for them with chocolate shaved into it. Radonna talked about every sweet thing Levi had said to her, and Rebecca mourned with her, until finally she took herself home.

On the way, Rebecca rode to the tor and climbed slowly to the Sitting Rock. She climbed like an old woman, stopping for breath on the way up.

She sat on the rock and wrapped her coat tightly around herself. She looked out at the old uncle and auntie mountains.

Where was he? What explanation? What of this picking up and shaking? This schooling? Was it meant to mean something? Was that the point? Was that the kindness, in the end? Was she expected to stop being a child of God and become a woman of God? Was she meant to stand and say, I carried this, I carried it, and I testify that I carried it? Was she meant to one day look at God and say, I am your child, I am royal, I have this to say, that I am royal. What you gave me I have loved. God didn't want her to be timid and shrinking. He wanted her to stand, to know her worth, her infinite destiny. Sitting and sunsets were one thing, but you knew him, really knew him, in the sorrow and in the serving. She understood that now.

She supposed she had always known that beauty and innocence would not protect you from the hard world. She knew it whenever she saw buffalo skulls dry and white in the prairie grasses. She knew it whenever she saw the silent Bloods standing in the town, imagining that she saw in their eyes the ghosts of the long-ago prairie: the grouse like black clouds weighing down whole trees, the buffalo herds covering the prairie like a people, like an offering of the earth, the rivers half water and half fish, all ghosts now, haunting.

Levi had been a good man. Someone would be in his house, taking care of things, the laying out of the dead, the supper for those who would attend the funeral, which was everyone, the care of the horses. Everything would be done for Levi that could be done, as if the dead cared about an orderly house, or what quilt he was wrapped in, or if the chickens had fresh water. But her people were in the beginnings and the endings. They were in the births and the deaths, the weddings and the times of sickness, the worship and the dancing, the weeping and the laughter, the work and the singing. They would do what they could.

Levi and Kincaid and Abigail were gone, but Rebecca was the ghost. She thought she could put her hand through every solid thing. The mountains looked shadowy, weightless. The prairie was breathing, swelling up, sinking down, as if it were an ocean and not earth, a swelling and shrinking sea.

If ever she had wanted another Sit with God, it would be now.

She spoke out loud to him.

"You were here, once. I saw you. You looked at our cows."

The prophets might have felt this way for a few minutes, she guessed: For a little while everything had made sense and you knew everything was going to be all right. And then it was over and God was gone and you were back to needing and fearing and fighting to live, and all you remembered of that good feeling was that you had been a part of something unutterable.

She heard something, and turned.

Of course he wouldn't be here. He would be walking the shores of creation, his feet wading in the firmament, considering suns, contemplating worlds —

"Coby," she said.

"Rebecca," he said.

He sat on the Sitting Rock beside her.

They were quiet a time.

"I have to say I've never prayed so hard as when you were sick," he said. "Not even in the blizzard."

"I remember," she said.

He reached into his pocket, pulled out a piece of paper, and handed it to her. She took it in her hands.

It was a land deed, for this quarter section of land.

On it was Coby's full name, Jacob Jeremiah Webster, and also the name of . . . Rebecca Eliza Leavitt.

"Coby, what have you done?"

"I bought it outright. It's ours—yours—to do with as you want. You don't have to prove up, or anything."

She held the deed before her with two hands.

In that moment, she became aware of the space between her heartbeats, a pause so brief you couldn't actually die in it, though you could fall down and down into it and find nothing familiar down there.

"But what will your future wife have to say about finding the name of Rebecca Leavitt on your deed?"

"Well, I hoped someday the two might be one and the same."

There was nothing between her and Coby now. No barrier, no wondering. He was asking her if she would tie up her life with his.

He turned toward the mountains, picked up a stone, and threw it hard. That stone had been here for thousands of years, she thought, and now it would be in a new place for a thousand years more.

"But if not, it's yours, no strings attached. I don't have any use for it because I have an idea, Reb. I also saved money enough to go to school. To college." He waited for her to think about that before continuing. "I've always thought it no more than a dream, to go to college. But coming here to the Territories, doing what I've done, it made me believe in dreams. It's made me believe in me. I've done everything I needed to do to prove up, and it was hard work, but I did the work. I'm not smart enough for college, but I can outwork them all. With a profession, I'll be able to pay my way and still keep my land, and grow nothing on it but buffalo grass. I'll sell my cattle and maybe someday an elk will come eat the grass."

"You are becoming a man of ideas, Coby," she said. "That could go well for you, or it could go badly. One never knows with ideas. What kind of profession?"

"I was thinking veterinary medicine. I'd rather take care of cows than eat them."

"Father will say you have no sense."

"That's what he'll say. But that's not what he'll think. He admires a man for doing what he thinks is right."

Rebecca thought she had inherited this trait from her father, for she admired Coby very much right then. She always had, but no more so than now.

She gazed out over the flats at the uncle and auntie mountains. "I've never told you why this is a special place for me."

Can you read my mind, Coby? she thought. You've known me, the real me, so long...can you read my mind?

"I heard you talking," he said, "I mean, before you saw me..."

She looked at him. Can you hear my heart, Coby Webster?

He threw another stone. It flew over the bluff like it might never hit the ground, into the shadows at the bottom, making no sound.

"It's just like you to go and see God when nobody else gets to."

"It was an accident, I think."

"What was it like?" he asked.

What was so strange about that question? she wondered. It took her a few moments to realize that it was the question you would ask if you believed.

"He was kind. Quiet. He didn't mind that I saw him."

Coby put his hands deep into his pockets then. He was looking at the sun perched on the tip of Black Bear Mountain, and his face was still.

She was gaining a gradual language, a way to understand herself talking to herself, a way to understand others. It was words that begat worlds: let there be light, I love you, you are just a little girl. Rebecca thought, be kind to yourself, in the grand scheme of things you are just a little girl.

She had done what she would, and what she could, and she had learned. She had learned that no mortal soul could love the whole world at once; you could love only the person before you, and the next and the next, one at a time, man by woman by child, just the one before you and the world each soul carried with her. That was grace. That was commandment. That was the Point.

"And yet, Levi, and Kincaid," he said. "Sometimes the world is just so damn sad."

She wanted to hold him right then, but somehow she knew she shouldn't. That wasn't what was required just now.

A bank of clouds closed over the mountains like a crown, a pronouncement.

"It's not fair, you know, that a single woman can't homestead," she said.

"I guess I know that."

"I mean to be a person, Coby. I mean to change what I can. I might not be the traditional kind of wife."

"I guess I knew that, too," he said.

They were silent a time.

"Are we getting married, then?" he asked.

"Weren't we always going to?"

He sighed and, after a moment, slung his arm around her shoulder. "You never let me be too sure. I'm relieved, Rebecca, I'll tell you."

They sat a long time like that, she, and Coby, and God.

AUTHOR'S NOTE

Thomas Rowell Leavitt, my husband's great-grandfather, traveled by covered wagon from Utah to the North-West Territories in 1887 with Charles Ora Card and some forty pioneers. They settled near Lee Creek in what is now Southern Alberta. Thomas and his family moved into the first completed log home by the river. In a year, the settlers would build a road to the timber, open a coal bed, build a church/schoolhouse, and fence in many acres. More settlers came, though some gave up and went back to the States. When later Thomas's house was toppled into the river in a flood, he resettled in Buffalo Flats, some distance from Lee Creek. He died of the flu, or, as they called it then, the grippe, at the age of fifty-six. His family recorded their memories of him, and wrote down the stories of their own lives in this new land.

Eventually these short histories were gathered into a hard-bound volume, edited and published by Dr. Clark Leavitt and his wife, Norma. This book is beloved to me for chronicling not only precious personal stories of family, but also a little-known but important part of the history of the North-West Territories.

My novel is a fictional story, peopled with characters of my own invention but for a few historical personages, including Charles Ora Card and his wife, Zina, Charles Magrath, Elliott Galt, Kootenai Brown, and Joe Cosley.

True also is the story of the building of the canals that were to be the means of bringing many settlers to this part of the North-West Territories. In 1889, Charles Magrath negotiated, for an irrigation project, the sale of thousands of acres of land to the Latter-day Saints, who had experience irrigating the deserts of Utah. Magrath was land manager of the North Western Coal and Navigation Company. The irrigation contract was canceled because of protests by those who despised the religion of the Latter-day Saints and thought they were going to overrun and take possession of the land. In my fictional story, the canal work goes ahead anyway. In reality it didn't go ahead until 1898.

Thomas married two wives, Ann Eliza Jenkins and Antoinette Davenport. When Antoinette died, he married Harriet Martha Dowdle. He brought Harriet to Canada with him, and Ann Eliza stayed behind on their farm in Wellsville, Utah. In 1890, Wilford Woodruff, president of The Church of Jesus Christ of Latter-day Saints, issued the Manifesto, which marked the beginning of the termination of the practice of plural marriage. The issue of plural marriage is not addressed in this story for the simple reason that it was not mentioned in any of the personal histories in the Leavitt "big red book."

Most of the personal histories spoke of poor but happy childhoods, of marriages, births, deaths, triumphs, tragedies. Many spoke of the push for survival, to "get along," as they called it, in this new land. There was the sense that this settlement was the fulfillment of the dreams of generations, the fulcrum upon which everything would change for future generations. Theirs were simple stories of family relationships and hard work, ending when they were stricken with age or illness, saying how good life had been.

Community events like dances and dramatics, box socials and Dominion Day celebrations, were always part of these life histories, and truly did knit hearts together and help people survive and thrive in an unforgiving and isolating land. Some incidents in my fictional story are based on real events, including the caramel apples plus one, Joe Cosley hiding his two-thousand-dollar diamond ring in a tree for anyone who could find it, and the story of milk for hay. Because my story was inspired by these real-life histories, I have indulged myself by giving the main character the last name of Leavitt, though she is not based on a single real person. It should be mentioned that not only did the settlers not winterkill, they eventually bought out the 10,000-acre Cochrane Ranche.

Babies who come too soon and men who abuse their wives are the work of my own imagination and did not appear in the records, which are consistently uplifting and chronicle a stoic, even humorous, take on challenges. Possibly my Leavitt ancestors did some sanitizing of the past in their record—not because they were trying to be false, but because it simply wasn't done, when pen came to paper, to complain or to dwell on matters that were best left un-dwelt-upon. When I would ask my father-in-law, Dean, the grandson of Thomas Rowell Leavitt, how he was doing, he would answer, no matter his troubles, "Better than I deserve." That was the prevailing attitude: difficult things happened, but you took them as they came, worked hard to overcome, and counted your blessings out loud. I have done my best to reflect, in my story, this clan culture.

ACKNOWLEDGMENTS

Thank you to all my brilliant children and children-in-law, who are skilled first readers and beloved best cheerleaders.

Thank you to dear friends Valerie Battrum, Dr. Chris Crowe, Elizabeth Crowe, P. G. Downes, Tim Wynne-Jones, Kathi Appelt and Cynthia Leitich-Smith for timely counsel and much-needed encouragement.

Thank you to the supportive and gifted community of students and faculty at Vermont College of Fine Arts who have inspired and taught me for over twenty years, and who believed in this book from the beginning.

Thank you to my High River Ward family, who have taught me so much about love.

Thank you to Ginger Knowlton, agent extraordinaire.

I am so grateful to my genius and long-suffering editors, Margaret Ferguson and Shelley Tanaka. I wore them out with this one.

Thank you to the Canada Council for the Arts and the Alberta Foundation for the Arts, who, as it turns out, are real and lovely people who care deeply about the arts.

231

Thank you to the late Dr. Clark Leavitt, and his wife, Norma, for the labor of love that became the big red book.

Thank you to my husband, Greg, for making me a Leavitt.

Thank you to God for beauty and language and story, and for His infinite patience.